TWISTER

Ten Days in August

Mary Jane Forbes

TWISTER
Ten Days in August

Copyright © 2012 by Mary Jane Forbes
All rights reserved. No part of this book may be used or reproduced by any means, graphic, electronic, or mechanical, including photocopying recording, taping or by any information storage retrieval system without the written permission of the publisher except in the case of brief quotations embodied in critical articles and reviews.

This is a work of fiction. All of the characters, names, locations, incidents, organizations, and dialogue in this novel are either the products of the author's imagination or are used fictitiously. The views expressed in this work are solely those of the author.

ISBN: 978-0-9847948-3-6 (sc)
Printed in the United States of America
Todd Book Publications: 8/2012
Port Orange, Florida

Author photo: Ami Ringeisen
Photos: Bigstock

Books by Mary Jane Forbes

FICTION

Murder by Design, Series:
Murder by Design – Book 1
Labeled in Seattle – Book 2
Choices, And the Courage to Risk – Book 3

Novel
The Baby Quilt ... *a mystery!*

Elizabeth Stitchway, Private Investigator, Series:
The Mailbox – Book 1
Black Magic, An Arabian Stallion – Book 2
The Painter – Book 3
Twister – Book 4

House of Beads Mystery Series:
Murder in the House of Beads – Book 1
Intercept – Book 2
Checkmate – Book 3
Identity Theft – Book 4

Short Stories
Once Upon a Christmas Eve, a Romantic Fairy Tale
The Christmas Angel and the Magic Holiday Tree

NONFICTION
Authors, Self Publish With Style

Visit: www.MaryJaneForbes.com

Forward

"TORNADO ON MY MIND
Got to protect my family and now is the time.
When lightning strikes and thunder booms,
I'll be sitting with peace of mind
In my TWISTER SAFE ROOM.

When that big wind starts to blow
where will you go?
In a sturdy room, that is what experts say.
A bath room,
A bath tub or a closet in the hall where you keep your broom?
When that roof starts to go and you're ducking flying debris,
I'll be sitting pretty in my TWISTER SAFE ROOM,
Custom built Just for me."

By Jeremy Davis

"…When deadly twisters chewed through the Midwest and South in 2011, thousands of people in the killers' paths had nowhere to hide. Now many of those families are taking an unusual extra step to be ready next time: adding tornado shelters to their homes.

Generations ago, homes across America's Tornado Alley often came equipped with storm cellars, usually a small concrete bunker buried in the backyard. Although some of those remain, they are largely relics of a bygone era. And basements are less common than they used to be, leaving many people with no refuge except maybe a bathtub or a room deep inside the house.

Safe rooms feature thick steel walls and doors that can withstand winds up to 250 mph. They are typically windowless, with no light fixtures and no electricity — just a small, reinforced place to ride out the storm. Costs generally range from $3,500 to $6,000.

The downside of public shelters is getting there. Even with improvements in twister prediction, venturing out into a rapidly brewing storm is perilous."

By HOLBROOK MOHR, JIM SALTER And PHILLIP RAWLS | *Associated Press, Sun, Apr 29, 2012*

Dedication

*To Enos Davis and his son Jeremy,
entrepreneurs designing and producing
safe rooms for those caught
in the onslaught of a twister.*

TwisterSafe.com

Acknowledgements

Enos Davis, TwisterSafe.com: a wonderful entrepreneur who shared many stories about the people his safe-room saved when everything around the unit was swept away. Thank you, Enos.

Thank you, Tom Cook, a survivor, for sharing your story.

Linda Trotter – thank you for sharing your family's love of music especially the violin.

Reviewers once again came to my rescue: Roger and Pat Grady, Lorna Prusak, Vera Kuzmyak, Molly Tredwell.

The Author

The following three inspirations stayed with me as I wrote *Twister*:

1. My own holiday tree that came into being when I retired to Florida. My grandchildren came to visit at different times of the year, the first being Easter which brought Easter bunnies, butterflies, and decorated egg shells to the tree.

2. The horrible twisters that swept from the Midwest to the East Coast in 2011 and 2012. Because of these natural disasters I found Enos Davis in an Associated Press article. That was a lucky internet search.

3. The sweet story of Min Chong, my Korean immigrant and his son Richard, fictitious characters, inspired by a conversation with Linda Trotter at a dinner party.

TWISTER

Ten Days in August

Prologue

February 2, 1942

On the second day, of the second month in 1942, two babies were born in the same hospital two hours apart. A boy and a girl. The two sets of parents, separated by less than two miles, had never met.

The babies grew up, knew of each other as they progressed through the school system, but were not what you would call friends. At the age of twenty, accounting students matriculating at the same college, they sat next to each other in Accounting 102. Mortimer's dark brown hair brushed the scale's height bar at five-foot-ten, and Jane, a petite five-foot-four, was known for her flaming red hair and blue eyes. When Mortimer caught sight of Jane that first day in Accounting 102, he knew this pretty girl sitting to his right was going to be his wife.

Two years later they married—two peas in a pod. The pair took *living a frugal life* to a whole new level. Fearing a disruption in employment, they wisely joined different accounting firms. With a passion for numbers, they spent raucous hours watching the figures in their bank account multiply: accruing, doubling, and tripling. Their entertainment.

Such was the universe of Mortimer Haliday and his wife Jane. They would have welcomed an increase in the number of members in their family, but babies didn't come along and they accepted the fact with grace. When Jane's sister and her husband, Martha and Harry Stitchway, had a baby girl, they asked Jane and Mortimer to be little

Elizabeth's Godparents. At the time, the Stitchways lived in Florida and the Halidays lived in Oklahoma.

The Christmas after Elizabeth's birth the Halidays, never sure when her sister's family might visit with the tot, left their Christmas tree standing all year, and thus it became known as the holiday tree. A tree for all holidays. And so also began the gossip about *those eccentric Halidays and their holiday tree.*

From the beginning of their marriage, the frugal Halidays agreed they would live on Mortimer's salary and invest all of Jane's salary in building their fortune. So for the first time since their bassinets were side by side in the hospital nursery, they added a third element to their tidy lives: gold.

While Mortimer poured over the morning newspaper, Jane adjourned to her room precisely laid out for her hobby—crafts. Jane knitted little caps for babies in the nearby hospital nursery, and socks and sweaters for the troops fighting somewhere around the world or standing guard in the States. But she spent most of her hobby time creating decorations for the couple's holiday tree. Adding Uncle Sam one fourth of July, Jane pasted rhinestones as stars on the flag the little character hoisted on his shoulder. Then one day she replaced the rhinestones with tiny diamonds.

Reading about a wholesale diamond dealer in Oklahoma City, they thought gemstones might be an interesting investment. After visiting the establishment, they made arrangements with the owner that on a regular basis they would purchase a few diamonds but only stones of the highest quality: flawless, excellent clarity, color and cut. So diamonds were added to their growing collection of gold coins. Because the accumulation of coins was unwieldy, they began replacing the coins with gold bars as they became equal.

The gold bars grew in number.

In December of 1979, one of Mortimer's clients gave him a tip on a hot new stock going public in February—two months away. Mortimer and Jane discussed the idea of purchasing shares in the new company. They came to the opinion that they absolutely should invest in the new corporation, that it was ordained. And invest they did. While all of Jane's salary to date had been used to purchase gold, and occasionally a few diamonds at the end of every month, they now split her salary between the gold and shares of Apple Computer.

By the end of 1986, the value of their shares totaled over sixteen thousand dollars, and, wonder of wonders, the stock split two for one and continued to climb again in value. Champagne flowed with dinner that night. Being frugal, it was a small bottle and the least expensive at the local liquor store. They agreed it had a wonderful taste and loved watching the lively bubbles.

Over the years, the Halidays had vacationed in Port Orange with the Stitchways, her sister's family, and had decided on a development of manufactured homes as the perfect place to retire. When the time came they picked out a home, a lot that it would sit on, and sealed the deal to move in two days after they started their retirement. It was perfect—frugal at $95,000. They bought the house—spacious with vaulted ceilings, skylights, carpeted, and a carport. As was typical for this type of development in Florida, they owned their home but the lot was rented. Homeowner fees covered the maintenance of the common areas, as well as mowing of the homeowner's lawns.

In 2007, Jane and Mortimer retired and moved to Port Orange, Florida. They retired with a secret fortune of seven million dollars, known only to them and an anonymous online banker.

Just prior to the time of their retirement the top designer of the establishment, where they bought their gold and diamonds, fashioned gold diamond rings for the couple to replace their original, small, gold wedding bands. The craftsman excitedly showed the couple a drawing of a man's unique gold, diamond-studded bracelet with black enamel. Price: $155,000. Jane insisted the designer create the bracelet for Mortimer, but it had to be one of a kind. After all, why squirrel away *all* the gold and beautiful stones when you could wear it and admire its beauty every day.

Jane had grown close to her niece. Elizabeth was now a grown woman and had settled into a career as a private investigator opening an office in a strip mall near her mom and dad.

After the move to Florida, Mortimer continued to enter on a weekly basis the spot price of gold and the Apple Computer stock price into their investment spreadsheet. He also printed a copy of the spreadsheet for the journal he kept in a three-ring binder. His entries were meticulous, detailing their growing wealth until Mortimer's death two years ago.

Two weeks after her beloved Morty died, Jane, now seventy and feeling poorly without her soul mate, decided she had to pull herself out of the doldrums. She marched into a beauty shop and asked the woman to apply a pink tinge to her silver hair. After the first blow dry, Jane wasn't satisfied. She wanted more pink in the color mixture. The beautician complied with her client's wishes for a second application. Jane left the salon three hours later, a twinkle in her eyes, and a decided pink glow framing her face.

Chapter 1

August 1, 2012

It was a steamy summer morning. Nothing special. Hot, muggy, sunny days were the norm for August in Port Orange, Florida. Jane sat in her living-room rocker, fanning her face with a piece of junk mail from a Chinese restaurant as she tapped her foot on the floor, the rocker slowly moving back and forth.

Her mind wandered as she gazed at her holiday tree, so pretty, the dark green boughs against the creamy-white walls. She thought the little characters on her tree looked a bit wilted, same as she felt from the heat. Only GumDrop, her orange tabby cat, didn't seem to mind as it lay purring in Jane's lap. Jane absent-mindedly stroked GumDrop's fur.

She hadn't turned on the air conditioning. It was only ten minutes after seven. She favored the quiet of the morning without the constant drone of the AC motor, preferring instead the slight murmur of the overhead fan.

The NOAA weather radio had kept up the warnings most of the night. That was the problem living close to the ocean. NOAA broadcasts continually alerted everyone of an approaching storm. *Don't they realize that most of us on land without a boat and aren't interested in hearing about fifteen-foot waves many miles out in the Atlantic,* she thought. *No! They just keep up the warnings.*

GumDrop snuggled deeper into Jane's lavender seersucker robe covering her matronly body of seventy years. The radio crackled with another NOAA broadcast filling the still, heavy air.

Jane smiled. Today she was going to Mabel's house to have her hair touched up. Mabel kept Jane's hair in a lovely tint of pinkish-silver, rather bouffant in style—just below her ears sweeping softly around her face.

Again NOAA crackled.

Jane frowned at the small, hand-cranked radio. She couldn't turn it off because it just flipped to battery power. The thought of taking the batteries out to shut the darn thing up never occurred to her because Mortimer had warned her never to do that. "When you live in the tropics you just never know when a bad storm will pop up from nowhere," Morty admonished when she asked if they couldn't take the batteries out for just a few hours.

Jane rested her head on the high back of the rocker. *Dear Morty,* she thought. *He always took such good care of me. Gone two years now, actually two years this month.* She missed him terribly but found solace in all the little creatures they had purchased for their holiday tree.

Every year since they were married, putting up their first Christmas tree, they both felt terrible when January arrived and they pack away all their friends in various boxes. But that changed when Lizzy was born. From then on the tree remained standing, decorated, with little white lights providing a soft glow at bedtime.

Dear Morty. Such a smart man. He toiled for hours at that accounting firm outside of Tulsa, as did I where I worked. No one knew that we were amassing a fortune. "Those Halidays live such a frugal life," she said mimicking their co-workers as she stroked the tabby's head.

"Oh, GumDrop, we had such fun. But then there was the day that one of his clients babbled on and on while Morty filled out the man's tax return. 'Apple Computer,' the man had said. 'This was the stock to own.' I tell you, the very next day we walked down to Fidelity Investments on our lunch break, opened an account, and made our first purchase. Six-thousand dollars," Jane chuckled.

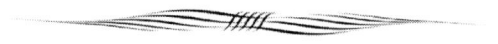

The Halidays' neighbors in Happy Days Estates, a manufactured home's park for people fifty-five-plus years of age, had no idea they were millionaires. Their stock certificates were stashed in a steel briefcase secured with a combination lock in the couple's safe-room. They had easy access to the certificates, selling a few from time to time. Just before they moved to Florida, they liquidated the bulk of the shares. Time to take some profits.

When they moved from Oklahoma to Florida they were surprised how cheaply they could live yet have all the comforts of a home to fit their lifestyle. After choosing Happy Days Estates as the place where they wanted to settle, they purchased a new double-wide home from a dealer in Jacksonville, Florida. They picked out a lot to rent, a four-inch cement slab was poured to accommodate the house and a safe-room. Too many of their friends in Oklahoma had lost everything they had, or worse yet, their lives in the seasonal tornadoes that tore through one southern state after another. Morty had insisted they install a safe-room.

After the slab was poured, the house was set in place, and the Twister-Safe was delivered and bolted to the cement slab. The Halidays quickly enclosed the safe-room in a nice garden shed at the end of the carport, out of the prying eyes of nosey neighbors. The shed went up so fast that nobody was the wiser that the structure housed a room made of steel.

After Morty died, Jane was terribly lonely without the companionship of her dear husband. But the Halidays had selected Port Orange to be near her sister Martha, and her husband Harry Stitchway, a policeman turned security guard before he retired. The Stitchways' daughter Elizabeth, a vivacious woman, became a private investigator, taking after her father in the area of law enforcement.

Jane loved her niece, as did Liz love her eccentric Aunt Jane. In fact, many thought Liz took after her aunt more than her own parents—crazy red hair and a confident strut.

Liz doted on her aunt, visiting her often. On Wednesday evening the pair played cards—poker or gin, downed a bottle of wine, once Liz was old enough to drink, and had a gay old time.

Nothing interfered with *Wine on Wednesday* with Aunt Jane.

NOAA crackled again, warning of a storm coming up from the south. The weatherman said it looked like the storm might converge with another bad weather system moving in from the north-west, a storm that had spawned several tornadoes on its path from Oklahoma, to Mississippi, and now heading toward Alabama and the panhandle of Florida.

Jane looked out her screen door. Nothing sinister in sight. The sun was shining, not a cloud in the sky, and Mr. and Mrs. Cardinal were having breakfast at the birdfeeder swinging in a slight breeze.

As early morning melted into the noon hour, NOAA crackled to life now and then, and a few clouds drifted overhead as Jane donned a fresh, flowered housedress for her hair appointment. Fastening the clasp of her single-strand pearl bracelet, she smiled at GumDrop asleep on her bed. Giving her kitty a pat on the head, Jane told GumDrop she'd be back in a couple of hours and ambled out the door and up the street to Mabel's salon located in the park.

It wasn't really a salon, but several ladies in the park were extremely happy when Mabel had a shampoo station installed with a swivel chair screwed to the floor. Her patrons sat in front of the vanity, mirror above, watching her snip, or brush color onto their graying hair. Mabel always liked it when it was time for Jane's color. Jane was the only one who dared to try different mixtures. She had settled on light pink after Morty died.

Strolling up the tree-lined narrow street, live oaks with numerous strands of Spanish moss adorning the branches, Jane was happily anticipating her appointment and catching up on the latest park gossip. She didn't notice the thickening black clouds gathering overhead.

Walking behind Mabel's home, Jane pushed opened the backdoor. The string of little brass bells jingled as she entered.

Mabel, a chunky sixty-six-year-old widow, was finishing Harriet's comb-out and the women exchanged greetings. "There, dear, you're ready for that anniversary dinner with your husband tonight," Mabel said twirling Harriet around holding a hand mirror so she could see the back of her hair.

"How many years is it?" Jane asked.

"Forty-two," Harriet giggled. "My mom said it wouldn't last a year. I guess I showed her. Thanks, Mabel. See you next week." Harriet shoved two ten-dollar bills into Mabel's palm. "A little extra today, Mabel. Treat yourself. Bye, Jane." Smiling, Harriet scooted out the backdoor and Jane settled into the chair at the sink waiting to be lathered up with Mabel's strawberry shampoo.

Mabel tested the water like a baby's bottle on her wrist and then doused Jane's hair. "Looks like rain," Mabel said massaging Jane's scalp. "Getting really dark outside. You may have to stay for tea until it blows over."

"Oh I couldn't do that. GumDrop's afraid of thunder. I brought my rain bonnet."

After the shampoo, Mabel slipped into a blue smock, prepared the color, and carefully brushed the mixture through Jane's hair. She then fixed two glasses of iced tea, poking a sprig of mint and a wedge of lemon into each glass. The pair chatted waiting for Jane's color to take.

Mabel didn't have much gossip today so she turned on the radio. The local weather lady was warning that there was a shift in the storm's direction and looked to be heading east.

"Residents in Volusia County should stay tuned for the latest bulletins but it would be wise to batten down the hatches, so to speak. Get your lawn furniture inside and anything else that might fly around. The winds are picking up. While we haven't spotted any rotations as yet, it is a possibility because the two storms are on a collision course over the middle of Florida."

"Let's get you rinsed and roll those curlers in case you want to make a run for it," Mabel said toweling off the excess moisture. She picked up the blow dryer switching it off after a few minutes leaving Jane's hair a little damp, and then winding strands around the jumbo yellow curlers.

Suddenly the room became very dark. The weather lady's voice boomed from the little red radio on the vanity.

"A tornado has been spotted on the ground in Port Orange near Clyde Morris Boulevard. Take shelter immediately. Interior room. Bathtub. Put a mattress or pillows over your head. Now!"

"Oh my God, Jane. That's just a few blocks from us. What should we do?" Mabel stood frozen, fear gripping her face.

"Come on, Mabel. We're going to my safe-room."

"No. No. I can't go outside."

"Yes, you can." Jane grabbed Mabel's hand, dragging her out the door. The two women ran down the street Jane's curlers bouncing as her feet hit the pavement, the towel and cape around her shoulders flapping. They turned into Jane's driveway, into the carport. Jane pulled opened the shed door, pulled open a steel door, shoved Mabel inside.

"I have to get GumDrop. Stay here. I'll be right back."

Jane ran the few steps to her back door. Opened it. GumDrop darted out into the bushes. Jane screamed for her to come back but GumDrop was out of sight.

GumDrop was gone.

Horrified, Jane ran to the iron box, stepped inside, and pulled the door shut. The safe-room had two seats attached to opposite walls facing each other. Jane reached under her seat for the flashlight she kept there and turned it on.

Mabel and Jane sat facing each other, knees touching.

"I can't breathe," Mabel whispered. "Are we going to die?"

Jane snapped off the light. Seeing the fear on Mabel's face was too scary. It was better to be in the dark. "Take deep breaths. There's cross-ventilation from slits in the door and the ceiling. Calm yourself, Mabel."

Chapter 2

Wednesday, August 1 – Day One

At precisely 2:23 p.m. the sound of a freight train barreled toward them.
Louder and louder it came.
Something struck the side of the iron shelter.
They heard glass breaking, metal banging against metal, a terrible crash against one side, then the other.
Wind howled, screaming around the outside of the safe-room, licking at the sides, slamming debris again and again against the steel.
Jane and Mabel felt for each other's hands and began to pray.
"Please, please, God, keep us safe," Jane whispered.
Over and over again they prayed for God's help as the noise became deafening. Their ears popping.
Then just as suddenly it receded.
Then it was quiet.
Only their raspy breathing echoed in the chamber.
"Is it over?" Mabel whimpered still holding Jane's hands in a death grip.
Both women were shaking violently but their breathing slowly ... slowly ... slowly ... returned to normal.
"Should we look outside," Mabel whispered.

"I don't know. Do tornados double back?" Jane asked.

"I never heard that," Mabel whispered.

"Why are you whispering?" Jane asked.

"I don't know. I'm scared."

"OK, I'll push the door open. Just a crack." Jane twisted the handle, pushed against the door. It moved a half inch but no more. A sliver of light fell across the steel floor. "It seems to be stuck. Come on, Mabel, let's both push."

The door didn't budge.

"What's that smell," Mabel asked. "Gas?"

"I think so ... and dirt?" Jane said.

"Does anybody know about this room?" Mabel asked. "We need help. Must be stuff blew against the door."

"My sister's family. Lizzy, my niece. They know," Jane whispered.

"Oh, my foot hit something," Mabel said. "Oh, God, Jane, is there an animal in here? A snake's going to bite us?"

"Stop it, Mabel. Nothing is in here but you and me. There's a metal case under your seat same as mine. I keep ... I keep important papers in here."

"You have important papers in here? This room ... a vault ... just for papers?"

"No, Morty ordered this room and had it installed when we moved from Oklahoma. He wasn't taking any chances after he read about hurricanes and tornadoes that had crisscrossed Florida. We keep a few papers in here."

Jane began wringing her hands. *I've done something really bad. All but two of the cases are in the house. Why didn't I wait until summer was over before cleaning in here? Oh, Morty, forgive me. I wasn't thinking.*

They heard the wail of sirens coming closer ... then receding.

"No one's coming to save us, Jane."

"Let's try to shove the door again. On the count of three push with all your might, Mabel."

"There's no room to really get an angle on the door," Mabel said. "I'll sit on the floor. Push with my feet against the wall and press my back against the door."

"OK. I'll straddle you and push with my shoulder," Jane said. "One ... two ... three. Push."

The door didn't budge.

"Jane, we're trapped. We're going to die."

"No, we're not.
Lizzy will come.
I know she will.
I pray she will," Jane whispered.

Chapter 3

Wednesday, 3:40 p.m. – Day One

The line of cars snaked slowly along Clyde Morris Boulevard, paused, driver's gawking through the trees where the tornado had reportedly twisted through Happy Days Estates.

Liz, following in line, suddenly jerked the wheel leaving the snake, parking behind a television van. The news crew was filming a report describing the scene. A policeman, his head ducked down, was talking to a distraught older man through his car window. The man was pleading for entrance into Happy Days.

Two squad cars blocked the entrance and officers were asking for identification, taking down names. If the person was not a resident or looking for a relative, they were instructed to move on down the street. Few were allowed access and those who were had to be escorted on foot. No cars allowed.

Liz checked her watch. 3:40 p.m. It was less than an hour since she had seen the television news report, had seen the first glimpse of the devastation in and around where her aunt lived, and only a little over an hour since the twister hit the ground changing the lives of the residents at Happy Days forever.

Climbing out of her car, Liz looked over at the officers directing traffic and talking to drivers through car windows. With hands on her hips she strode toward the entrance to the park. The oppressive humidity dampened her black short-sleeved shirt and trousers causing them to cling to her body. She yanked the useless clip from her hair, allowing her shoulder-length auburn hair to fall around her sweaty neck. She felt her body lurch fearing that she wasn't going to find her aunt alive.

Liz turned toward the pillars that once held an arched sign over the park entrance—Happy Days? Not likely.

"Liz?"

Hearing a man call her name, she turned as the man's fingers closed lightly around her arm. A touch. A lifeline of support. Help.

She looked up into the face of a friend, her brown eyes softening as his dark eyes drew her to him.

"Manny, thank God you're here. My aunt ... my aunt's in there. I have to find her."

"You can't go in there, Liz. It's not secure. The gas guys shut off the area but the power company hasn't given the all clear. There are live wires—"

"No, Manny, I have to go in, now." Liz pulled away but the police captain reached out and grabbed her arm, this time with a firm grip.

"What street did she live on?"

"Sunnydale."

"OK, but, Liz, you have to hold my hand. Watch every step you take. Nails are sticking up from boards, shards of glass can cut through your shoes ... and ... watch the wires." Manny turned toward one of his officers. "Fred, what's the word from Florida Power and Light?"

"Hang on, Captain."

The officer flipped open his cell, held it to his ear as he stepped away from a car, the driver's head craning for a better look out of the window.

"Captain, FPL says they shut down the transformer. There's no power in the park. It's clear."

"Thanks. I'm taking this lady to check on her aunt's house. Keep in touch."

Manny turned back to Liz, grasped her hand. "OK, let's go. But I warn you it looks like a war zone. The men in hazmat suits up ahead are looking for survivors in the rubble, or... people who didn't make it."

"Manny, you don't understand. My aunt may be hurt, trapped, but I know she's alive."

So sure she was right, her eyes pleaded with him to hurry, her hand tugging him along.

Manny shoved a recliner out of their path a piece of aluminum impaling the seat cushion. As he pushed the chair a clump of dirt fell onto his arm, another down onto his black pants.

Picking their way up two short streets, Liz could see ahead that Sunnydale had taken a direct hit. The homes on both sides of the narrow street were leveled. Liz tried to run but Manny held her hand tight as they continued to pick their way through the debris—a refrigerator on its side, carports gone, cars upended and tossed like toys into the next neighborhood. None were left standing on their wheels. Torn aluminum sheets, razor sharp, pierced clothing, bedding, and pieces of furniture. Tree trunks were splintered like toothpicks, or, if they managed to remain standing, were stripped bare of leaves and bark.

A Red Cross team of three was administering first aid to an elderly couple. A rank smell of gas permeated the air mixing with the scent of moist dirt.

"Where was your aunt's house?" Manny asked.

His question, his words, stuck in her throat. "There, over there. Oh, my God, look. Look, Manny."

Manny put his hands to his forehead shading his eyes.

An iron container gleamed brightly in the sunlight, the beams of light cradling the structure.

Liz yanked her arm free of Manny's grip and scampered, zigzagging through the debris, sidestepping nails protruding up at her through splintered wood, pieces of broken glass sharp enough to cause skin to bleed. She screamed as she approached the iron shed and then began banging on the steel door. "Aunt Jane, Aunt Jane, are you in there?"

Liz stopped banging, her first raised, holding her ear to the tiny crack in the door. Did she catch a muffled voice?

"Lizzy, Lizzy, we're here. Thank God you came," Jane yelled. "Lizzy, I can't open the door." From the outside Jane's voice was muffled but Liz knew that her aunt was alive.

"Wait a minute. There's a stove lodged against the side of the door," Liz said pushing under Manny's arms to help shove the dented chrome stove out of the way.

Underneath the stove was a splintered bookcase, a twisted computer tower, and alongside it a blue toilet bowl—not a scratch, sparkling clean.

Jane, pushing against the door from the inside at the same time Liz and Manny pulled it open, fell into her niece's arms.

"Are you hurt?" Liz asked holding her aunt up as her legs began to buckle.

"No, dear, I'm okay. A bit shaky is all. Who's this," she asked looking up at the six-foot officer, hiking up his gun belt.

"My friend ... Captain Salinas. We go back a few years," Liz said throwing a quick smile in Manny's direction.

Mabel, holding tight to the edge of the safe-room door, stuck her head through the narrow opening, tears streaming down her face.

Manny saw her peeking out and quickly stepped forward. "Here, let me help you," he said taking the woman's arm so she could step to the side of a nail-studded board.

"Lizzy, this is my friend Mabel," Jane said her voice shaking. "She was fixing my hair when we heard the warning. I dragged her down here."

"Where do you live, Mabel?" Liz asked looking into the stricken woman's face, her blue smock as fresh as when she put it on this morning.

Jane and Mabel looked up, dazed, at what had once been their street. For the first time they saw the complete destruction—all the houses that had stood on Sunnydale were gone. Debris covered the entire area blurring the lines where streets, sidewalks, and lawns had once been.

Mabel began sobbing. "My house ... my house is gone." She pointed off in the distance. There was nothing left in the direction she was pointing her quivering finger except mounds of treacherous rubble. Her legs gave way and Manny held her in his arms, preventing her from falling on a piece of twisted aluminum.

Sirens could be heard in the distance along with the occasional sputtering of a chain saw. They could only wonder about their neighbors. Surely they didn't all make it.

"Let's get you both out of here," Liz said slipping her arm around Jane.

"No. GumDrop ... she may be hurt."

"Who's GumDrop," Manny asked.

"My tabby. She never goes outside but when Mabel and I ran to get in the safe-room she darted out the door. Ran into the bushes ..." Her words slipped away as she looked where the garden had been.

"Aunt Jane, she's probably too scared to come home now. We'll come back later to look for her."

"Can you tell one of your officers about GumDrop?" Jane looked up at Manny, a tear meandering down her cheek.

"Of course," Manny said nodding.

The Red Cross team picked their way to the group standing by the iron shed. "Hi, there. I'm John, this here is Cindy and Carol. Are you two okay?"

Jane, wisps of her pink hair poking out from the remaining curlers, covered with a brilliant flowered beautician's cape, and a white towel around her neck, faced the Red Cross members.

"We're quite all right, thank you," she stammered. "My friend and I came through without a scratch, just a little disoriented. I'm Jane and this is Mabel."

"We brought you a couple bottles of water," Carol said handing them each a bottle.

John stuck his head and shoulders halfway into the iron enclosure.

"I'm Jane Haliday's niece," Liz said looking at Carol. "And this is Captain Salinas. He helped me find my aunt."

"We've met the captain before," Cindy said with a smile as she extended her hand to Manny. "Mind if we take a look inside, Jane? That's some tank you have there. Saved your lives I reckon."

John backed out of the structure holding two metal cases as the other two Red Cross volunteers, prying the door open further, poked their heads through the opening. Cindy stepped inside.

"I guess you want to take these cases with you," John said handing one to Manny as Jane grabbed the other.

"Oh, mercy, yes. All my … all my … all my important papers are in them," Jane said. Shading her eyes from the brilliant sun, Jane scanned the field of debris looking for something glistening in the sunlight, her other four cases. She had stupidly taken them in the house while she cleaned inside the shed the day before. The day before—years ago.

"Manny, can you tell your officers that I have, rather had, four more cases just like these two. They're very important … papers … papers my late husband put in the cases for safe keeping. Papers … memories of my dear Morty."

Chapter 4

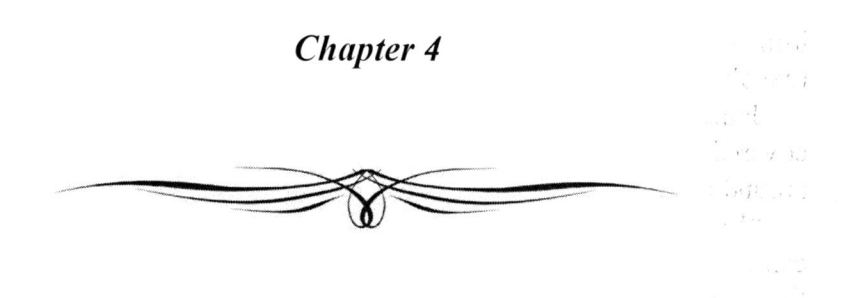

Wednesday, 4:45 p.m. – Day One

    Star Bloom sashayed down the street to the little room she had rented for the summer on the ocean side of Daytona Beach. She was working up a sweat under the heat of the blazing sun, even now in the late afternoon, almost five o'clock. The angry black clouds of a few hours earlier had rumbled out to sea leaving clear blue skies.

    Her feet were killing her. The lunch crowd had been particularly heavy at the Manatee, a bar facing the sandy beach and the lapping waves of the Atlantic. A twister had skipped along about four miles to the west and thirsty patrons swelled in the establishment thinking they would be safer at the bar than at work. Fortified with pitchers of beer, lunch soon became happy hour with special cocktails decorated with tiny red, yellow or blue umbrellas stuck into various colored fruits depending on the concoction. The fleeing workers took advantage of the never-ending weather alerts, hunkering down while the twister hop scotched north to Flagler County, leaving devastation and heartache in its wake. Some debris landed in the Manatee parking lot as well as along Atlantic Avenue.

    Star's tips had been sparse until she began serving the second and third round of drinks. Then the crowd loosened up, especially after the first television crew showed pictures of what was left of Happy Days Estates.

The owner of the bar called in reinforcements for the evening crowd and told Star to go on home for a few hours. He needed her back rested and ready to flash her radiant smile, ignoring the occasional fanny pinchers. The twenty-five-year-old blonde was his best waitress. She was genuinely friendly, liked by both men and women, garnering her a continuous stream of tips as the drinks flowed.

"Get back here by nine o'clock," he bellowed as she swept out the door into the hot, humid air.

Star was thrilled when she found the room for rent. It was on the back, west side, ground floor of a two-story house that had been converted into cheap rentals for the numerous service staff employed by the hotels, motels, bars, and restaurants around Main Street, the street where all the action occurred along the beach.

Her pace quickened when she rounded the corner to her building, down the path along the side to her private entrance. Kicking off her high heels, she released her long blond hair from the black ribbon at the nape of her neck and dropped down on the green leatherette beanbag near the patio door. She closed her eyes but they popped open again. The sun, low in the sky, was hitting her in the face. Struggling to her feet, she took a step, reached for the twine to draw the drapes shut but something bright struck her in the eye through the fronds of a palmetto bush at the back of the narrow lot, not more than fifteen feet away.

She looked closer her nose almost touching the glass.

"I must have worked harder than I thought," she mumbled. "That sure looks like a doll in that bush."

Star pushed the sliding glass door open and walked barefooted across the grass, her eyes glued on the object. She dropped to her knees, leaned closer to the bush, cocked her head.

Grabbing for the doll, it clung to the prickly side of the frond. The main stalk had grown out at an angle with several fronds from the base branching in different directions each sprouting clusters of fronds. Crouching lower beneath the thick palmetto bush, Star pulled the doll free.

There were several splotches of mud on the doll's dress, so Star held it away from her short, black mini-skirt. She couldn't' get her skirt dirty because she had to wear it again when she returned to the bar for the night shift.

"Why, you're a Christmas angel," she said softly, smoothing the angel's blond hair back in place. Still kneeling she reached into the bush again retrieving the angel's halo snagged on the tip of a frond.

"Look at that, little angel. Your halo is a diamond ring. It's really wide, thick—a man's wedding band. Wonder if it's brass. Probably gold," she said examining the ring.

"Oh, my God, if it's real gold it could be worth a lot of money. Maybe fifty dollars. More with the diamonds," Star giggled. "You are my lucky angel," she whispered putting the ring on her thumb. She was careful to keep her thumb bent because the ring was so large it could fall off. It was much bigger than her finger. *Must have been a really fat man,* she thought.

Picking up the Angel, keeping her thumb folded, she trotted back to the sliding door in case someone was spying on her from the other windows.

Exhausted, Star put the angel and the ring, on the little round bistro table she bought for five bucks at a consignment shop. She washed her hands and face with cold water in the bathroom, and then flopped down on her blow-up-mattress. Bone tired, she instantly fell asleep.

Chapter 5

Wednesday, 4:50 p.m. – Day One

A little before five o'clock, employees, cutting out of work early, turned on their radios for the latest news on the twister that had bounced through Port Orange and Daytona Beach, continuing on up the coast. The storm that had spawned the tornado left flooded streets and pools of standing water in its wake—puddles and wet parking lots. Steam curled up from the pavement as the sun beat down on tourists and residents alike. It would be another three hours of blistering heat before the sun would disappear in the west.

Kelly, a young mother, her brown curls long gone due to the humidity, guided the grocery cart out the automatic plate-glass door of Publix supermarket to her car. She had picked up her daughter from playschool and the little four-year-old sat in the elevated seat of the cart, dangling her sneaker-clad feet through the holes. Facing her mother, the little girl leaned forward, arms outstretched, head down, watching the spray kick up from the cart's wheels as they rolled through the puddles.

"Mommy, look. A ballerina doll. Look," she squealed reaching for her mother's arm, tugging for attention.

"Hmm."

"Mommy, stop!"

"Where," Kelly asked her eyes following her daughter's finger pointing two cars back that she had passed.

"There. Mommy, please get her."

"OK. I see her." Kelly backed up the cart to where the little ballerina laid under the bumper of a red sedan. Picking the doll up, she brushed the dirt from her pink ballet skirt. "She's kinda dirty, honey."

"She's beautiful. Look at the diamonds on her tutu. It's sparkly like mine, Mommy. And pink. Can I have her, please, please?"

"I doubt those are real diamonds but they sure are sparkly as you say." Kelly reached around her little girl and dropped the doll in the sack with the eggs. "Let me clean her up when we get home. If she looks okay, you can have her."

The little girl smiled up at her mommy, accepting her solution, as Kelly pushed the button on the car-door opener releasing the trunk's lid.

At the other end of the parking lot, Gary, a thirty-something man in jeans and a gray T-shirt, splashed through a puddle in his sandals pushing his grocery cart holding two cases of beer and several large bags of chips. At the passenger side of his white truck he punched the button, pulled the handle down opening the door. He shuffled a couple of feet to the side of the cart, reached in for the top case of beer and hauled it onto the floor of the front seat. Scooching over a little to get a better grasp of the second case, he felt something brush against his foot.

Looking down ready to kick away whatever it was tickling his right toe, Gary saw a nutcracker man, a policeman nutcracker, his uniform painted black, and a lady doll dressed in a black pantsuit. Their arms were linked together. He picked up the dolls and had a thought. *Rose loves miniature dolls and she collects nutcrackers. Someone's loss is my sister's good fortune. I'll clean them up for Saturday's party. Oh, oh, the nutcracker's jaw is broken.*

Gary looked around the pavement, squatted, peering under the truck. "There's your cracker," he mumbled reaching for the broken sliver of wood. Standing up, he pocketed the little piece of wood and set the two dolls on the front seat. "I'll glue your jaw back and then you'll have a new home with a big family—Rose's dolls."

Hearing the click, click, click of a pair of high heels, Gary turned and gazed at a pretty woman in a pale-yellow summer dress dodging the puddles with her cart. With a chuckle he climbed into his truck, pulled forward, and drove out of the parking lot.

Karen missed several more puddles as she marched to her car, opened the driver-side door, threw her keys on the seat, and began transferring her groceries onto the backseat. She glanced up at the sound of somebody honking. The ruckus didn't seem to be targeting her so she turned back and finished unloading her cart.

She closed the car's backdoor and returned the basket to the stall with iron rails corralling the empty carts. Propped up against the rail, a doll, about five inches tall, long red braids, smiled up at her. "Well, aren't you the cutest thing," she said picking up the doll. "I had a Raggedy-Ann like you when I was little. Mom embroidered eyes on her just like yours. You, my little good-luck charm, are going home with me."

Smiling, Karen brushed the dirt off the doll's green bib overalls with several rhinestones on her pocket, and green ribbons tied at the end of her pigtails. Sliding in behind the wheel she sat Raggedy Ann on the seat beside her, the rhinestones sparkling in the sunlight. Turning the key in the ignition, she carefully backed up, and left the parking lot.

Chapter 6

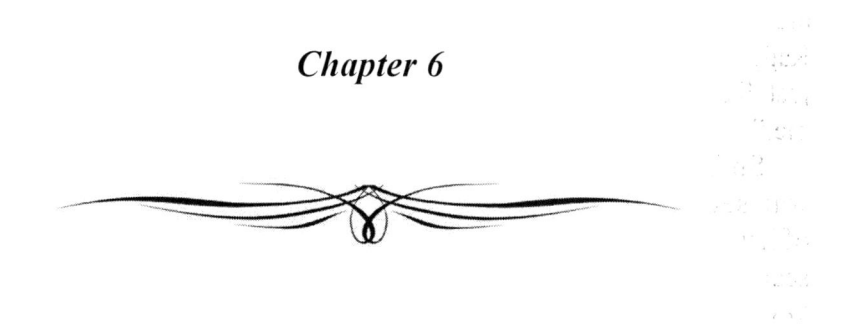

Wednesday, 5:00 p.m. – Day One

During the last two hours poking through the rubble, Jane and Mabel spoke softly, hugged and cried with neighbors walking by like robots. Liz, always by their side, went along on their emotional ride. They had begged Manny to let them stay awhile. Sighing, he nodded, gave each a hug, and returned to his officers at the entrance.

Jane and Mabel clung to each other when they saw Harriet's husband being escorted away—Harriet was found dead.

With her toe, Jane lifted the corner of a dark-red velour cushion she had never seen before. Sucking a quick breath, she stooped and carefully pulled a small picture frame from its hiding place beneath the cushion—Morty smiled up at her.

"We have to leave," Manny said striding up to Liz. "Dozers are coming to clear the street. Where's Mabel?"

"Red Cross, Cindy helped her to her house … where it was," Liz said. She glanced at her aunt, then back to Manny shaking her head.

Manny stepped to Jane's side, put his arm around her shoulders. "You have to leave. The city is urging residents to wait … tomorrow or the next day to comb through the debris. Volunteers are bringing cartons. They'll help you."

Jane lifted her face to Manny. A tear dropped from her chin onto the flowered beautician cape. She turned around the picture frame she was clutching for Manny to see.

"Your husband?"

Jane nodded.

Mabel called to them as she tiptoed around the hazards in front of her. She was waving a fur stole—fox.

"I see," Jane called, grinning under her tears. "That's wonderful. I found my Morty." Jane looked at her niece. "Mabel loves that stole. A gift from her husband."

Liz, a metal case in one hand, held her aunt's arm leading her away from the iron box that had saved her life. Following closely on their heels, Manny, holding the other case, grasped Mabel's arm as they made their way out of the park.

A line of cars continued to snake down the street passed the park's entrance, drivers still trying to get a glimpse of the destruction. Now, close to six o'clock, the twister was long gone and the storm that had spawned it was out to sea.

Liz helped Jane into the front seat of her silver PT Cruiser as Manny assisted Mabel into the back seat. Liz took the case from Manny's hand and placed it, along with the one she had carried, onto the back seat next to Mabel.

"Here, Lizzy, give them to me," Jane said.

"OK, but there's room—"

"No, dear, please, hand them to me. They're very important ... papers ...papers Morty put in the cases for safe keeping. Papers ... from Morty."

With the ladies safely ensconced in Liz's car, Jane's arms squeezing tight a case on each side of her, Manny turned to Liz. "She must have loved your uncle a lot the way she's clinging to those cases."

Maggie, Liz's black and white Border Collie, dusted the grass furiously with her tail as Liz untied her. Free, she leaped into the car next to Mabel and then over the seat to the back. Her head thrust forward giving Mabel a welcome slurp on the ear. Mabel swatted in the dog's direction but remained mute staring ahead.

Manny stepped up to Liz taking hold of her shoulders. "You okay?"

"Have you ever seen anything like this?" she asked, touching his arm. Feeling his strength, she straightened her shoulders under his grip.

"Once. Hurricane Andrew. Several of us from the department went immediately to Miami to help stop the looting."

"Looting? Nothing left here to loot."

"You'd be surprised at what will be found ... but only tokens of their life before this twister."

"Aunt Jane and Mabel seem to be holding up ... still..." Liz glanced at her car. "I'll call my mom to let her know I'm bringing her sister home with a friend. Let them rest a bit and then make some plans on what to do. When do you think they can sort through the debris for anything that might be of value?"

"The city's making plans. Maybe tomorrow. I'll check and let you know. They'll try to open a path so residents can look through what's left without getting cut. If not tomorrow, I would hope by the next day. I'll call you."

Liz looked up into Manny's eyes. He was several inches taller and muscular as ever. He smiled down at her, his eyes filled with compassion. "It's good to see you, Liz. Glad you still have your dog," Manny chuckled, glancing at Maggie, her head out the window. She gave a soft whine. Liz had checked her several times over the last few hours but the dog was anxious to get moving.

Smiling, Liz looked over at the squad car. "I see Peaches is still riding shotgun with you."

Peaches, Manny's black Lab, head out the window, was also anxious to get moving.

"Oh yeah."

Turning into her parent's driveway, Liz parked behind her dad's car under the carport. Their development was similar to Happy Days Estates but newer, the homes larger.

The screen door banged open as Martha Stitchway ran out, took one look at her older sister and gently wrapped her in her arms. Liz helped Mabel out of the car, Maggie darting out the open door as Mabel stepped onto the driveway.

Harry held the front door for the women, called to Maggie, and followed the dog inside.

Jane and Mabel plopped down on the flowered-chintz, slip-covered couch, sighed and looked at Martha, then looked at Harry, and then Liz. Martha and Harry, sitting on chairs facing the two homeless women, leaned forward, concern written on their faces.

"Jane, you're alive. It's a miracle you and your friend survived," Martha said softly, reaching for her sister's hand.

"We wouldn't have but for Jane's quick thinking and that … that iron room," Mabel said.

"Sorry, Mabel, my manners," Jane whispered, barely able to talk. "This is my sister, Martha and her husband Harry," she said, patting Mabel's hand. "And, this is Mabel, my hair dresser and very good friend." Jane reached up and began removing what was left of the rollers in her hair letting them drop into her lap. Jane untied the back of Mabel's blue smock helping her slide it off.

Mabel slid closer, slipped the towel away from around Jane's neck and then untied the flowered cape revealing Jane's cotton housedress. Rolling the curlers up in the cape, she managed a smile and then looked up at Martha. "Can I use your phone? I'd better call my daughter. It's almost dinner time so she should be home. Works at the CVS on Nova Road. Gets off at 5:30."

"Of course," Martha said. "Come with me, there's a phone in the kitchen. How about a nice cup of tea? Or a soda?"

"Tea would be nice," Mabel said trailing after Martha to the kitchen.

"Make that two will you, Martha?" Jane said as she struggled to get up off the cushy couch.

Liz, leaning against the wall behind her dad, watched her aunt, wondered how she was coping with what had just happened to her. Quickly stepping to assist Jane, Liz held her hand as she shuffled into the kitchen.

"Turned out Morty knew what he was doing when he insisted on that safe-room," Harry said following the others. "Your sister and I shook our heads at the time. Thought he was crazy. Crazy like a fox, that Morty."

Mabel hung up the phone and sank onto a chair Martha had drawn up to the kitchen table. "Good thing I called. She had just switched on the TV. Started crying on the phone. She'll be by in about ten minutes. Elizabeth can you call her cell? I said you'd give her directions."

"Lizzy, I have to go back tonight … GumDrop may be looking for me," Jane said, worry lines filling her face, her voice gaining strength.

"I asked Manny when you might be allowed in the park. He thought possibly tomorrow or the day after. Not tonight. It's too dangerous."

"Now, Lizzy, you call that nice captain and tell him I HAVE to get to my place no later than tomorrow morning. Poor little GumDrop. She was so scared. Never been outside."

Liz pulled her cell from her pants pocket, handed it to Mabel to punch in her daughter's number and she handed it back to Liz. Liz gave the girl directions and tried to reassure her that her mother was safe and unharmed.

The tea kettle whistled, the tea made, and served.

No one said much. The yellow walls, pine cabinets, red linoleum floor held the sad-filled kitchen. Too many questions to be asked and no energy to give any answers.

Martha put on a pot of water to boil for spaghetti. It was going to be an easy dinner tonight—pasta out of the box, marinara sauce out of a jar, salad out of a bag, and a bottle of red wine to soothe everyone's frazzled nerves.

Mabel's daughter arrived. They tearfully hugged, then stumbled to the car, and drove away. The story of the ordeal in the iron-room would wait to be told.

Liz set the table as her dad poured the wine.

"I've lost everything," Jane mumbled pulling a hanky from her pocket. "All my little friends on the holiday tree, everything that Morty had so carefully saved for us. I have nothing. Lizzy, I have to find GumDrop." A gush of fresh tears filled her red eyes.

"We'll try our very best to find her, Aunt Jane. If she's not at … at your house, we can put up posters on the fence outside of the park. I'll ask Manny where I can call if someone at the department picks her up. I'll also leave word at the two vets in the area."

"You'll stay with Harry and me while you get yourself situated again," Martha said setting the salad bowl on the center of the table.

Jane sighed. "Gone. Everything gone."

"Not everything, Jane. Your bank wasn't hit by the tornado. In fact, after it tore down your street it skipped up to Flagler County, touched down once more, at least that's according to the news reports, and that was it."

"Everything we owned was in the house except for the two cases you brought in from Lizzy's car, Harry."

Martha looked sharply at her husband, then back to her sister. *How was that possible?*

Chapter 7

Thursday, 6:00 a.m. – Day Two

A sunbeam shot through the boat's portal striking Manny across the face. Blinking, he opened his eyes, rolled over to look at the clock. 6:01 a.m.

Thump.

Peaches' front paws hit the bed, followed by a whine and a soft bark.

"Yeah, I hear you. Can I have two more minutes?"

An insistent bark and a fast trot to the bedroom door, said, no way to two more minutes. Peaches wanted out for her morning run.

Manny rolled his legs over the edge of the bed, bent his head down, dragging his fingers through his thick black hair, rubbing his scalp, then his moustache. Another day protecting Daytona Beach citizens. Twelve years on the force. Twelve years plus four months. His spirit was flagging and he wasn't sure why. He liked his job. Found it exciting. But lately … lately he didn't have the same verve to chase down the bad guys.

"Maybe I'm just getting old, Peaches," he said reaching for his black jogging suit. Every piece of clothing he owned was black. He drew his running shoes from under the bed where he tucked them yesterday. A quick trip to the bathroom, a swish of mouthwash, and he was ready to start another day.

Trotting down the four steps off his boat, he jumped to the dock. Peaches was already running up the driveway. Manny smiled at his dog and then frowned. The image of two poor souls, staring dazed, scared, bewildered at the remains of their property popped into his head. He shook the picture from his mind and began jogging down the road. The sweet smell of dense vegetation, the singing birds and bright sunshine began to lift his spirits as it did every morning. This was something he could depend on.

Peaches chased a squirrel, watched it run up the trunk of a large oak then sat on a branch chirping, teasing her. Losing interest, Peaches scampered on down the road, passed Manny and began barking as a black and white dog emerged from the opposite direction.

It was Maggie, Liz's dog. Manny smiled as the sight of the auburn-haired woman came into view. She was sitting on a boulder on the side of the road, sketching something in the dust with a long stick. Liz rented a small cottage a mile east of Manny's houseboat, but on the other side of the street. They used to run into each other jogging but that ended almost a year ago. Both had altered their jogging schedule and had lost touch until yesterday.

Liz looked up as the barking dogs approached, followed by Manny. Her hair was drawn back into a tight ponytail, her brown eyes appearing even larger. This morning those brown eyes were hollow, but she managed a faint smile.

Manny pulled up beside her, bent over, hands on his knees as he sucked in a couple of deep breaths. He took note of his friend. She looked pathetic.

"I'd say good morning, but you look like you don't agree. What's wrong?" He stood in front of her, hands on his hips waiting for an answer. *Except for yesterday, how long has it been since I've seen her? And why?* A pang of loneliness filled his chest. He stepped away, looked to the sky, fingers locked behind his head. Dropping his arms, he turned back to her.

Liz was shielding her eyes from the sun that peeked through the leaves.

"It's a good morning—no black clouds on the horizon, no wild wind blowing houses down," she said. "Yeah, I'd say it's a good morning. On the other hand, Aunt Jane says she lost everything yesterday and my appointment book is empty. My business is in the dumpster. No one wants to investigate these days, I guess."

"Well, let's start with your aunt. How is she?"

"When I left her last night she and my folks were finishing off a bottle of wine. She's petrified that her furry companion, GumDrop, was killed yesterday, or, if she wasn't, that GumDrop won't be able to find her way back home because she's never been outside and there's no home to return to."

"What you need is a *strong* cup of my ship's coffee. Come on young lady, up on your feet." Manny took the stick from her hand, threw it in the woods, and pulled her to an upright position. "We have to get the spark back in that hot temperament of yours. It seems to have fizzled. A redhead without fire in her belly is no redhead at all. A fake."

Liz let herself be pulled up and kept stride with Manny as they walked back down the road, his arm around her shoulders. Maggie and Peaches, noting the change in direction, ran after their owners and dashed ahead of them.

Liz had been on Manny's boat once before. She was working a case in conjunction with the improper handling of Arabian horses and needed his help. At the time she was nursing her wounds over a failed relationship. He didn't notice her, or, if he did, she was too bruised to respond.

Taking the four steps up from the dock two at a time, Manny turned and extended a helping hand to Liz. Peaches had already leapt aboard. Maggie waited for Liz and then trotted up the steps behind her.

"Galley's this way," Manny said taking three quick strides to a door and a staircase leading down. "Watch your head."

"I remember. Almost knocked myself out the last time you invited me to have coffee with you." Liz gazed out the galley window at the river while the coffee perked. Nothing like what she imagined it looked like yesterday during the storm. Today the tide pushed the water gently in from the ocean. Manny set out the cream and sugar then filled the mugs.

"I like your kitchen. Your galley. It's cozy and your right the coffee is strong." Taking another sip she noticed out of the corner of her eye that the dogs were lying out on the aft deck soaking up the sun, exhausted from the run and resting up for the next one.

Manny sat at the table opposite Liz, fingering his cup, then his moustache, staring into the steam curling above the coffee.

"Looks like we both require a *strong* cup of ship's coffee. You're a little droopy, too," Liz said leaning back, staring at the man across from her. She had always thought him impressive. Obviously fit, muscles bulging to be released from under the fabric of his black T-shirt. A moustache had never impressed her one way or another. His was a brush over his upper lip, and along with the thick black brows, added to his character of a don't-mess-with-me lawman.

"You said your calendar wasn't exactly filled with investigations," Manny said, looking up into her brown eyes. They didn't seem to look at him, but deeper, into his soul. "Things are … well … seem different for me, too. Don't get me wrong, we're busy—crime is up because so many are out of work, downturn in the economy I guess—but it's not the same. We've had cutbacks at the department. Everyone's working long hours. We don't have the time or the manpower to finish an investigation before we have to hand it over to the lawyers. I don't get the same satisfaction anymore rounding up the criminals."

"You aren't thinking of quitting the force are you?" Liz asked. She didn't realize she had reached across the table until her fingers touched the top of his hand. His hand—it was large, wisps of black hair on the knuckles. Her hand jerked back.

Manny's eyes followed her action and reaction.

"Tell me about your aunt."

"Other than GumDrop, I was surprised at some of the words Aunt Jane used to describe her situation. After all, I can't believe she's destitute. She's definitely in shock. I know Uncle Mortimer's retirement check—"

"Mortimer? I don't think I've ever known a Mortimer. That's some name," Manny said chuckling.

"I know," Liz laughed with him. "Probably why we always called him Morty." They locked eyes—a warm understanding look, over smiles, between friends.

"Not sure what she means when she says that she lost everything that Morty had set up." Now it was Liz's turn to finger her cup. "Manny, can you help Aunt Jane get into the park today so she can check if GumDrop came back?"

"I'll say, yes, but let me call you."

Chapter 8

Thursday, 6:55 a.m. – Day Two

The tide rolled in pounding the Port Orange shoreline. It was after daybreak and the seagulls and pelicans cawed out in hunger, diving into the water for their breakfast. The cacophony penetrated the thin clapboard siding of the motel room, at the end of a string of rooms. It was the only motel that remained standing in a row of motels resisting the bulldozer's blades since the 2004 hurricanes. The owner, knowing his building would be torn down sooner or later, left the various rooms of chipped, lime-green walls and scratched furniture as is. Why paint—here today gone tomorrow was his philosophy.

Johnny Blood pulled the pillow over his head but the noise of the crashing waves and the starving birds pierced the thin foam. Rolling over, he checked the other bed to see if his pal had managed to stagger in during the night. Johnny had left Benny in the bar around 2:00 a.m. Benny Stupend was having himself a fine time with the scantily clad barmaids until they found he was all talk and no cash.

Tired of the scene and anxious, Johnny had left wondering when the next batch of drugs was coming. He was on the bottom rung of the gang. Hell, he wasn't even on the ladder but he had big plans to move up that ladder. Show the big boys that he could play along, that he could be trusted. He only endured Benny's presence for comic relief. He gave Benny a job now and then but never divulged what he was really up to. When you were a member of a gang you didn't talk about serious stuff, like how he got a sudden fistful of money. A friend today could shoot you in the back tomorrow.

Benny was passed out on the bed still wearing what he had on at the bar—cowboy boots, jeans, and a red NASCAR-500 shirt with Dale Earnhardt standing next to his 88 car.

Johnny rolled out of bed, dressed in his cargo pants, picked up his truck keys, and left the room he had occupied for the last month. The owner was more than happy to give him a cheap rate if he stayed and paid by the month. Many tourists remained up north away from the Florida heat, not that any tourist would be caught dead in this dilapidated establishment.

But the place was perfect for Johnny, a place where he could lie low. He chuckled. He was lying low, about as low as you can get.

He stepped out of the lime-green dungeon and onto the white sand, pulled his Miami Dolphin ball cap down, the bill shading his blue eyes from the sun climbing higher over the horizon. Picking up a shoot of grass, he sat on his haunches watching the birds performing cannonball dives into the water. A couple of pelicans swooped down but pulled up at the last second, soaring into the sky, riding the breeze.

The morning surf was heavy, waves building, breaking, only to build into another. Johnny used to enjoy surfboarding, riding waves like the ones this morning, his sandy hair turning blond from his days on the beach. He watched, mesmerized by the show in front of him.

The building surf twinkled in the bright sun.

A flash of light hit Johnny in the eyes.

Blinking, he followed the wave.

Something shiny was caught in the wave.

He stood, watching the wave roll in.

The shiny thing rolled up onto the sand pushed by the thundering wave as it hit shore.

Barefooted, Johnny ran to see what the shiny thing was before the retreating water carried it back out to sea. He snatched it out of the water and then scurried away from the jaws of the receding surf. Sitting down on the sand he examined the case he had grabbed. It was heavy. Made of steel. Brinks Home Security was stamped in blue letters on the side near the hinge.

Johnny shook the case. There was definitely something inside. The case had a combination lock. In Johnny's mind, if something was locked that meant someone didn't want someone else to see what was inside. The lock only fueled Johnny's determination to find out what this person didn't want him to see.

Johnny looked out over the water. The noise was deafening, particularly when the waves resulting from yesterday's storm crashed ashore. Case in hand, Johnny hustled to his pickup truck. Unlocking the truck, he reached underneath the driver's seat and pulled out his revolver. Jamming the gun into the waist of his pants, he pulled his T-shirt over the handle and hustled back to the beach.

With his back to the motel, the case lying on the sand in front of him, he waited for the next wave to crash and then aiming at the lock pulled the trigger.

The bullet pierced the case blasting the lock apart. Stuffing the small pistol into the leg pocket of his pants and flapping the tape together, he sat on the sand pulling the case up between his legs. He lifted the lid.

Two gold bars gleamed up at him. Gleamed, even though the lid of the case shaded the bars from the sun. In the corner of the case was a small, black-velvet pouch. Johnny untied the braided gold string and dumped the contents into his palm. If he wasn't mistaken, and Johnny was rarely wrong, there were five diamonds in his hand of various sizes.

His heart began to pound.

There was a manila envelope covering the bottom of the case. It was not sealed. Johnny pushed the metal prongs through the flap of the envelope, pulled the prongs back from the hole, and retrieved several small booklets. Bank account registers. He was holding four bank-account registers. He ran his finger over the gold lettering of the bank name on the front of one of the rectangular, blue plastic books.

He quickly opened each book to see the ending balance. His jaw dropped. He stared bug eyed. One by one he added the balances in his head. *That can't be right. Nearly four million dollars?*

He looked at the front page of the books. Each had a yellow sticky note—a handwritten pass code, username, security question answer, each sticky different, to access the different accounts.

Lifting each sticky, his eyes focused on the page underneath. All were in the name of Jane Haliday.

A reward?

Naw. That would result in pennies on the dollar.

Johnny had to think. Had to plan. Actually, there was no time to plan.

He didn't know how this case floated into his hands but he felt it was destiny.

Maybe good old Jane is dead.

He had to act fast. Find out if he could access the account and transfer the money out. He was good at that. He'd been trained to hack into corporate accounts, but this, this was a private person giving him the pass code.

Then there were the stones. They sure looked like diamonds to him.

And, the gold bars. Anyone with the balance shown in these books could easily afford the diamonds and the gold bars.

"Don't rush and do something stupid, Johnny Blood," he whispered. *First the money. Then the gold bars and these rocks. Ask someone how much the gold is worth. These shiny stones. I'll go to a pawn shop. But I won't show them anything. Just ask a few questions.*

Johnny closed the lid, took off his shirt and wrapped it around the shiny case to hold it shut. Turning back to the motel and his truck, his mind continued to spin.

He had lots to do today.

First the bankbooks. He had to act fast. Act now.

Johnny drove his truck onto Atlantic Avenue, turned west on Dunlawton, and a few miles later turned into Panera Bread. A stream of workers queued up for their morning buzz and immediately left. Johnny slid into a corner booth with internet access. No one was around to bother him. No need to plug into the power outlet. He had charged his computer last night thinking about a report he had to type up today. He smiled. This was a story he was not going to type into the computer. He was going to drain the money before some family member of this dead person closed the accounts. No, he wasn't about to let that happen.

Accessing the first account took some time, but once he knew the routine he drained four million in less than fifteen minutes. He couldn't believe his eyes. This couldn't be happening to him, Johnny Blood. Johnny Blood voted the most likely high school graduate to make it big. He laughed. *There's big and then there's really big. Huge. Gynormous.*

He closed his laptop. Cradled it in his arms. A broad smile crossed his face. *Now don't get cocky, Blood. You can't let on to Benny what you found. Hell, you can't let anyone know. You still have a job to do. Earth to Johnny ... come back.*

Walking out into the brilliant morning sun, his step jaunty, he climbed into his truck. He had three more tasks that had to be done quickly. The first was to hit Wal-Mart to purchase a new laptop. Nothing fancy but good enough to hold him for awhile. Good old Wal-Mart. Always open.

Twenty minutes later he crossed the first task off the list in his mind and headed back to Panera Bread. Seeing that the booth he had used earlier was still unoccupied, he once again set up shop. Transferring the programs and data from his old laptop to the new one was done over one cup of coffee.

Bundling the two laptops under one arm, he tossed his empty coffee cup into the trash, and asked the young girl behind the food pickup counter if she had a large trash bag she could give him. He'd made a mess, spilling coffee on his papers.

Check off number two.

With the trash bag folded on top of the laptops, he pushed through the glass doors, and once again with a lively step walked to his truck. He stuffed his old laptop into the trash bag along with several balled-up pages from the morning paper. Driving out of the parking lot he turned right onto the access ramp, Interstate 95 North. Seven minutes later he turned off the interstate onto International Speedway. Traffic was heavy. Just what he had hoped for.

Crossing Williamson Boulevard, he turned into the Cracker Barrel Country Store. The parking lot was almost full.

Perfect.

He drove to the end of the line of cars and parked. Spotting a large dumpster several yards away, he waited a few minutes watching the kitchen help disposing of bags of garbage. A teenager, struggling with two large trash bags, shuffled to the dumpster and, with a mighty heave, threw the bags onto the pile. He returned to the kitchen.

Johnny emerged from his truck casually carrying a trash bag. At the dumpster, he too gave a mighty heave, his bag landing in the middle of a torn bag spilling soggy pancakes, eggshells, and crushed strawberries. Johnny returned to his truck, and drove back to his motel.

Check off number three.

Chapter 9

Thursday, 9:17 a.m. – Day Two

The door to the lime-green dungeon slammed shut followed by angry footsteps, then silence.

Benny Stupend rolled over, his bloodshot eyes squinting up at Johnny Blood glaring down at him, hands on his hips.

"Benny, where's the C-note you owe me?"

Benny blinked. "I don't have it. You know I was out ... barhopping last night. It was wild ... crazy ... everyone yakking about that storm."

"Yeah, and what did you pay the barmaids with, your good looks? Not!"

"No, I had money."

"My C-note?"

"No."

Blood's glare held Benny's wide-eyed, red-veined stare. There was no forgiveness coming Benny's way.

"Sorry, Johnny, but wait. One of my regulars, Hector, homeless guy, needed a fix. Said to hurry. He'd pay me. He was in bad shape, Johnny, or I never would have taken it."

"Taken what?"

"Hector lied to me. No money. The only thing he had was a pawn ticket. He jabbed it in my hand. Said it was worth more than a hundred. Guaranteed it. But the shop owner only gave him fifteen. He was closing up so Hector had to take it."

"Yeah?" Blood snapped, "and just what was IT?"

"I don't know, Johnny. He wasn't making sense. Said he found it. You take the ticket, Johnny," Benny whined jamming his hand into his jeans pocket, pulling out a twenty-five cent coin and the pawn ticket. "Here. The shops just a couple of blocks away."

"This does me no good, Benny. The ticket's made out to the guy who bought it … your customer. I don't have identification to match."

"Go now, Johnny. The owner doesn't come in until after two in the afternoon. The guy he has working in the morning is a bozo. Just tell him you left your wallet home. Tell him to look up your name. Not your name. The name on the ticket. I know my guy pawns stuff there a lot. There'll be a record. Bozo won't want to tick off a good customer. You know what I mean?"

"Yeah, okay, I'll give it a try. But if IT isn't worth more than a C-note I'll leave IT at the shop and you'll still owe me the $100 plus interest for the aggravation. And, Benny, get those muddy shoes off the bed and take a shower. You smell worse than this moldy room."

Chapter 10

Thursday, 9:29 a.m. – Day Two

Donald Sanderson glanced over his shoulder at his six-year-old daughter clinging to the sides of the rickety old Radio Flyer wagon. *What a joke—flight and radio.* He'd be thankful if his daughter could walk.

Bella smiled up at her daddy with her big blue eyes. *Always happy.*

Donald loved her so much. If only she could run and play like other children.

Isabella's mother died in childbirth leaving her husband to care for their daughter. He didn't know at the time that she was born with a birth defect, a defect that didn't manifest itself until she tried to walk. Her legs didn't work right.

At first it was thought her legs would get stronger but the opposite happened. The doctors recommended an operation be performed by the chief surgeon of the pediatric unit at the hospital. The operation could result in Bella being able to walk after extensive therapy and rehabilitation. But Sanderson had lost his job as an electronics salesman—cell phones, television, and computers—due to the recession. Without a job, and no insurance he couldn't pay for the surgery, an operation that would run well over $100,000.

He prayed every night for guidance, for a miracle. But days, weeks, and months past and the operation was put on hold. He prayed over and over for a job so he could pay for the operation that would give Bella a chance to walk.

Donald usually took Bella to the beach on Sunday after church, but it was so muggy and stuffy in the house he decided to take her this morning. Because of yesterday's storm, a large oak limb had fallen across the driveway blocking his car. But he could still put Bella in the wagon. He had sawed off the legs of a child's chair and bolted it to the base, retrofitting the wagon so she had support.

Pulling the Radio Flyer along the sidewalk, Donald had to stop several times to remove debris the little wheels couldn't roll over, throwing sticks, cans, and a window shutter to the side. He couldn't have pushed her in the wheelchair even if he wanted to and he wished he'd worn his sneakers instead of flip-flops. But, he didn't mind, the breeze kept them cool in their shorts and T-shirts and they had less than a half mile to the boardwalk leading down to the beach. Bella held tight, her eyes peeled ahead on her daddy's hand gripping the handle, her white floppy hat with a wide brim shading her sweet face.

Crossing the street to the small beach parking lot, Donald pulled the wagon onto a path and then up onto the boardwalk. The ocean sparkled ahead, the waves crashing onto the sand—the storm still raising havoc even though it was far out to sea.

Bella strained, leaning to the side watching the path disappear and the boards begin.

"Hold on, Bella, the boardwalk's rickety," Donald called to her as the wagon bumped onto the boards that led down to the beach.

"I know," she said holding tight to the sides but still looking over the edge, her brown curls with strands of gold bouncing at each crack in the weathered wood.

Ambling down the ramp, Donald slowed his steps as he approached the sand.

"Daddy, Daddy, look. An Easter egg." Bella leaned hard to her right. Donald followed her gaze as Bella shifted her weight pushing against the side to see the egg. The wheels hit the sand. The wagon jackknifed throwing Bella over the side.

"Bella, are you okay?" Cursing under his breath at the old shaky wagon, he scooted around after his daughter, but she was squirming on the sand to the egg sitting in the middle of some tall tufts of grass.

Now in her reach, Bella grasped the large green egg and rolled over on her back. Donald bent down and picked her up.

She held the egg up to her daddy, her blue eyes twinkling in the sunshine as he brushed the sand from her pink shorts and shirt, set her sunglasses back on her nose, and settled her in the wagon.

"Daddy, it's Eggbert. Oh, he's just as cute as his picture."

"Who's Eggbert?" he asked with a sigh, kneeling in front of his little girl thankful that she wasn't hurt.

"My favorite storybook. The one you gave me last Christmas. You remember. Eggbert—the cracked egg. But he learned that a little crack couldn't stop him. Like my legs, Daddy, just because they don't work now, I know they will sometime."

"Yes, baby, they will ... sometime."

Donald scooped a shallow hole in the sand, spread a towel over it, and set Bella in the indentation for support. She liked to build sandcastles and talked to Eggbert telling him how much she loved the beach and especially today because she found him—her very special new friend.

"Daddy, Eggbert looks like a duck. He has feet and a bill. But, he's happy. See, he's smiling. When I take my nap today can you put an extra pillow next to mine for Eggbert to sleep on. Please, Daddy. A pillow for my new friend?"

"Yes, I'll put another pillow on your bed when we get home from the beach so Eggbert can have a nap, too."

"Oh, thank you, Daddy." Bella smiled up at him and opened her arms for a hug.

It was soon too hot under the sun so Donald returned Bella to the wagon as she kept up the chatter with Eggbert planning what they were going to do today. They bumped along the boardwalk, then on the sidewalk, the road, and were soon home. A home that was the same as the day his wife died. A two-bedroom, old frame house, painted turquoise on the outside, and yellow on the inside.

Donald carried Bella in the house and she carried Eggbert shaking him back and forth to match her daddy's steps. He set Bella in her highchair that she continued to use to support her body, her bare feet dangling.

"There's something inside Eggbert's tummy. Listen, Daddy," Bella said shaking Eggbert, both hearing a muffled rattle from inside.

"Maybe Eggbert's having baby," Bella said looking up at her daddy. "It wants to come out. Can we see?"

"Let's have a look," Donald said setting a glass of milk on the highchair tray. Taking Eggbert from Bella's outstretched hand he shook the doll once. Raising his eyebrows at Bella, they both grinned. The curiosity bug struck father and daughter.

Eggbert's body was an oval about five-inches tall and almost the same width. His head and feet were made of soft rubber. There was a hole the size of Donald's thumb in the top. Eggbert's rubber head was wedged into the hole and his neck looked to have expanded so the head held in place. Donald pinched the little neck together and pulled Eggbert's head from his body. Turning the egg upside down, a folded tissue fell onto the tray beside Bella's glass of milk. Donald unfolded the tissue and a yellow stone rolled onto his palm.

They both blinked at the brilliance of the stone.

Picking it up, Donald turned it around and around in the sunlight.

Bella shook the egg to see if anything else was inside and then replaced Eggbert's head, her little fingers easily pushing his neck back into the hole.

Donald wasn't sure what he held in his hand, but he was sure he was going to take the stone to the jewelry store. The jewelry store where he had purchased the diamond ring for Bella's mother when he asked her to marry him. At that time, Bella was just a twinkle in his eyes.

Chapter 11

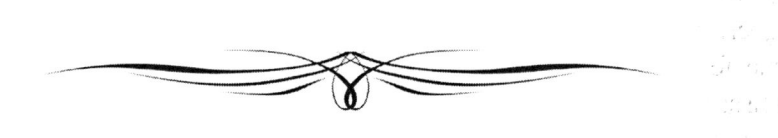

Thursday, Noon – Day Two

The morning news reports— radio, newspapers, and television— were grim. The twister had skipped around Port Orange then over Daytona Beach. The worst area to be hit was the Happy Day's park. Other than that it felled a few trees, then up to Flagler County touching down in a field, and then, thankfully, broke apart as the storm blew out over the Atlantic. Two people had died in Happy Days. One of the them was Jane and Mabel's friend Harriet. An elderly man, found hunkered down in his bathtub, was taken to the hospital in critical condition; five others were also treated at the hospital but were expected to be released by noon. Snowbirds owned several homes that were destroyed and were thankful they were spending the summer up north.

Manny had called during his various stops telling Liz he would meet her at the entrance to Happy Days. The bulldozers had cleared a narrow path so they could spend some time at the site sifting through the rubble.

By noon Liz had picked up her aunt, stopped at the liquor store for a few empty boxes hoping they would find some of Jane's valuables in the debris, stopped at Wal-Mart for a cat carrier hoping they would have a cat to rescue, and stopped at the automobile repair shop on Dunlawton. Jane's car was in the shop for service and missed being thrown around the neighborhood.

Jane paid the repair bill for the oil change and a new air filter. The service manager commented on how lucky she was that her car was in the shop when the tornado hit. She agreed that it was one piece of luck. Fifteen minutes later she pulled in behind Liz and parked. They retrieved the boxes and cat carrier from Liz's car. Liz had called Manny on her cell and he was waiting for them at the entrance. Both women were dressed to work in the dirty rubble—jeans, shirts, and sneakers. Jane's clothes were borrowed from her sister.

"Glad to see you took my suggestion about wearing sneakers," Manny said giving Jane a hug and Liz an extra squeeze. Smiling he took the boxes from Jane's hand. "Even so, watch your step. Especially look for nails coming up through pieces of wood ... and glass."

Manny held Jane's arm with his empty hand. He kept glancing back to Liz pointing out sharp objects.

When Jane saw the iron shelter that had saved her life, she pulled away from Manny's hand, hustled around him, and began calling for GumDrop. Hearing a faint *meow,* a bedraggled orange cat covered in mud, limping, her front right paw lifted off the ground, peeked around the side of the shelter.

"Oh, my baby. You're here. You poor dear," Jane cooed to her disheveled buddy. "Liz, look, she's here." Jane glanced up at Liz and Manny, tears streaming down her face.

Liz set the carrier on the ground, opened the wire door, and Jane carefully lifted GumDrop inside. The scared, exhausted cat did not resist. Jane poured a few drops of water in a saucer from her water bottle and set it in the carrier along with some cat nibbles in an olive jar lid.

Liz kissed her aunt's tear-stained face. "Do you want to take her to the vet while I start to look through this ... this mess?" Liz asked.

"Oh, yes, dear. Do you mind? It's just down the road. I'll be right back."

"You go ahead, and don't hurry. I'll call mom. She said she wanted to help sift through what's left. Is it okay if we stay awhile, Manny?"

"Sure, but don't wander around. Watch for those nails and broken glass," Manny said. "Tell your mom to identify herself to the officer at the entrance. Only residents are allowed in to search their property. I'll call in an hour, see how you're doing. Come on, Jane, I'll walk you to your car. Here, let me take that carrier for you." Grasping the carrier from Jane's hands he stopped, turned back to Liz, and with one arm gave her a quick hug. "Be careful," he said in a husky voice, his eyes seeking hers, and just as quickly he turned away taking Jane's arm, holding GumDrop away from his holster.

With a tingly feeling in her stomach, Liz watched her aunt walk carefully away under Manny's guidance, and then set about searching the stuff that lay around her. Her dad had given her his heavy-leather work gloves to protect her from cuts, and Liz hoped her jeans would protect her legs. Even though the temperature was approaching ninety degrees, she did as Manny suggested, and kept her long-sleeve denim shirt buttoned at the wrist. She didn't want to risk an infection from a cut.

In the first hour of her search she filled two cartons, including a picture of Morty and Jane the day they were married. The glass was broken but the picture was unscathed. She found a shoe and another picture of a party—a group of women she recognized who had lived down the street. A scrapbook was under a piece of aluminum in perfect condition. Liz opened the cover to find Polaroid pictures of the ornaments—little people, and souvenirs her aunt and uncle had purchased over the years for their holiday tree. *At least she'll have these pictures to remember her tree,* Liz thought.

Looking across the cluttered expanse, she saw small clusters of people, two or three, sometimes only one, doing what she was—digging to find pieces of their lives before the F3 twister hit their street.

She uncovered a drawer with a couple of sweaters, another drawer upside down—empty. Nothing from the holiday tree. A few pieces of bedding. It seemed that anything that wasn't in a cupboard was gone, picked up by the one-hundred-fifty-eight-mile-an-hour funnel of wind, and deposited … deposited where? Out in the ocean? In someone's backyard? Liz supposed her aunt could put a list of items she felt were valuable to her in the Lost and Found section of the newspaper just in case someone came across them.

Martha came and joined her daughter in the sifting. Jane returned. The vet said GumDrop needed stitches for a cut on her side, a splint tightly bandaged around her front leg, ointment on her scratched paws, and a bath. GumDrop was staying overnight at the clinic.

Manny called.

Liz told him they would be going home soon and asked him if they would be allowed back in for more scavenging tomorrow. Manny said, yes, and that in fact they only had tomorrow to sift through Jane's property. The city had scheduled waste trucks to begin cleaning up the site.

Also, Liz told him that for some reason her aunt wanted to talk to them privately and wondered when he could meet. Preferably today. "She said it was urgent. Something about the four missing steel cases."

"How about dinner, early? 6:00?" Manny suggested.

"Sounds good. Why don't we meet at my place? Give Aunt Jane and me a chance to clean up, and Maggie's going to need to get out of the house after being cooped up all day."

"Okay if I bring Peaches?"

"But, of course."

Manny thought he detected a slight lilt in her voice. "I'll bring a bottle of wine ... celebrate GumDrop's return."

Chapter 12

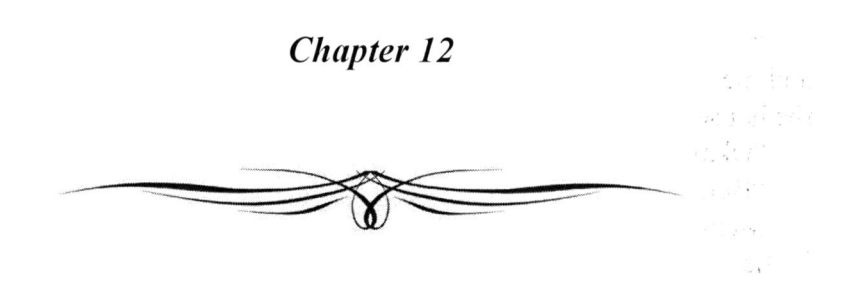

Thursday, 6:00 p.m. – Day Two

    The stubby white candle sat in the middle of the plain-pine kitchen table. The flames occasional flicker created the aura of a séance. The sun had slipped behind the forest surrounding Liz's house so the candle's flame began to call up shadows. Jane's eyes glazed over as if in a trance, her pink hair taking on a soft glow, her fingers pulling on her hanky. She had asked Manny to meet with her at Liz's house indicating there was something very important she had to tell them.
    Only them.
    She sat at one end of the table. Manny and Liz sat opposite each other. Peaches and Maggie were asleep under the table on the braided rug. Manny poured the deep red wine, a Florida merlot, into the mismatched wine glasses, leaned back, and stared over the flame at Liz. He raised his eye brows questioning. She responded with a slight shrug of her shoulders and a widened stare.
    Although Jane had asked to meet with them, she was at a loss as to how to begin, how to broach the subject she had asked them to hear. A tear meandered down her rouged cheek. She pulled a fresh hanky from her green-and-white-checked housedress, again borrowed from her sister. She hadn't ventured to Wal-Mart yet to buy new clothes, replacing those that had either blown away, were covered with mud, or hung shredded on nearby palm trees and bushes.

"Mortimer must be so disappointed in me," Jane whispered, her eyes held by a flicker of the flame.

"Why would you say that, Aunt Jane," Liz said, laying her hand over her aunt's fingers gripping the hanky.

"We had such fun posting the entries in our journals. I saved every one, you know," she said looking up at Liz.

"What kind of journals?" Manny asked taking a sip of wine.

"Our investments. We logged in everything. The journals are in a suitcase," she said looking wistfully at the candle.

"How big is this suitcase," Liz asked.

"Oh, not a suitcase, a briefcase. One that you carried out of the safe-room. Morty didn't want them to be too heavy for me, you know."

"Them? You mentioned there were more—more than four besides the two cases we removed from the safe-room?" Manny glanced at Liz. She shrugged her shoulders again, as bewildered as he was.

"There are six cases in all ... were six cases." Another tear slithered down her cheek but she quickly mopped it before it reached her chin.

"That's a lot of journals, Aunt Jane."

"Oh, my gracious, the journals are all in one case—older entries in some tablets ... most on computer CDs. The others, well, the other cases contained our mad money."

"Why weren't all the cases in the safe-room if they had money in them, or a safe-deposit box?" Manny asked.

Jane raised her eyes to him, seeking his understanding.

"We always kept them in the safe-room. 'Better than any bank vault' Morty would say. I was cleaning the safe-room. It had become cluttered, a convenient place to store stuff. I had taken everything out, finished wiping down the inside, took two of the cases off the dining room table and put them back in the safe-room. But I stopped because it was time to leave for my hair appointment with Mabel."

Jane looked back at the flame. "I'm sorry, Morty," she whispered.

"How much mad money are we talking about, Jane?" Manny asked.

Liz sighed. She and Jane showered after they came home from digging around in the debris. She felt better after dressing in clean black Capri's, white sleeveless blouse, jeweled sandals replacing the heavy sneakers. *This is going to take awhile,* she thought. *Prying information from her aunt has always been difficult. When Morty died, mom and I tried to find out about her financial situation. We wanted to be sure she had enough to live on. I asked her several times but she always waved me off, saying she had enough, saying that Morty had provided for their* retirement. God knows she never spent much, and they lived very simply in their Happy Day's home. But for the first time she seems to be concerned.

Liz pushed back her chair. "I'll get us something to nibble on. Manny? Cheese and crackers?"

He nodded and then looked back at Jane. "You mentioned money. Did you put cash in the cases?"

"Not really. One had stock certificates ... shares we hadn't sold. Apple Computer. We had such fun entering the end-of-the-week share price. On Sunday Morty would pour over the stock tables in the newspaper. The financial section."

"You kept the certificates? I thought brokers kept records, held the shares in your name," Liz said as she retrieved a brick of Colby-Jack cheese from the refrigerator and began cutting it into cubes.

"Well, yes. But at first, we wanted to keep them. Hold the paper in our hands ... felt like we really owned a piece of the company. You see, we lived on Morty's salary and always invested mine. All of mine. Morty had a tip from a very trusted client. We bought our first shares within a month after the company went public. What a bonanza that turned out to be." Jane looked to the ceiling, closed her eyes shaking her head.

"Over the years the value of the shares went up and up and up," she said chuckling. "Oh, we had a grand time. And when the stock split, three times you know," she smiled up at Manny then over to Liz standing with a box of crackers, mouth open, staring at her aunt. "Well, when it split, two for one each time, that was cause for celebration. I bought little gold stars to put next to the journal entries when that happened. Later when Morty transferred the journals to the computer, he'd highlight such a major event in yellow."

"If you kept the stock certificates you hadn't sold in one case then what was in the rest?" Manny asked.

"Gold. Bars and coins. Oh, we tried diamonds as an investment for a couple of years, but that really didn't give us a big bang for the buck—that's what Morty said. He always wanted the biggest bang for the buck."

"Aunt Jane, do you have any idea what kind of money you're talking about?" Liz asked. Her brows furrowed as she shot a look at Manny setting a bowl of crackers in front of him along with a plate of cheese cubes.

"Several million, Lizzy. But you must promise me you'll never tell," she snapped. "You see we kept what we were doing with our money a secret." Jane looked straight at Manny for his answer. After he gave her a nod, she looked beseechingly into the eyes of her niece. "Promise me? Not even your mother."

"Yes, I promise not to tell. But, Aunt Jane, you and Uncle Morty lived very simple lives—no big trips, no cruises, I don't remember you're ever taking a vacation. At least not before Uncle Morty died, and I haven't seen any change since then."

Liz plopped down on her chair, picked up her wine glass and grinned devilishly over the rim at her aunt. "I often wondered how we advanced from games of gin and poker at this very table to Wednesday nights at the Poker Club. It was after Uncle Morty died. After all those years of keeping journals you decided to kick up your heels, get out of the house, and I was a willing accomplice. I'm not a very good private investigator ... didn't put two and two together."

Liz chuckled, took a sip of wine and caught an astonished look on Manny's face.

"What?" she smiled. "We have a limit. Aunt Jane always staked us both—that was all we could lose. If we lost, we left. If we won ... well we played awhile longer." Liz looked quickly at her aunt. "You called it your mad money and that Uncle Morty would want us to have fun. You never let me chip in my own—"

"Of course not, Lizzy. You didn't have money to spare. I did. Besides, I always told you it was my way of bribing you to come with me on our WOW poker night."

"Excuse me, ladies, what's WOW?"

Jane and Liz giggled, the first sign Manny had seen that they were relaxing ... a little.

"Wine on Wednesday," Jane said. "Lizzy and I have a standing date on Wednesday night so don't you try to muscle in on Wednesdays with my niece, Captain."

Manny sighed. "I wouldn't dream of it. Although, I've been known to play a mean game of gin," he said putting a cheese cube on a cracker and handing it to Jane.

"What do you think, Lizzy. Maybe we should invite him. Once anyway," Jane said smiling at him. "Captain, can you bring that liquor box in here, the one with the scrapbook that Liz found."

Manny strode to the hall. The dogs looked up, saw he wasn't going out the door and laid their heads back down. "Is this what you want?" he asked holding up a thick binder on the top of one of the boxes.

"Yes, that's it. Thank heavens it didn't fly apart ... memories of my holiday tree." Jane sighed. "I'm a little tired. A glass of wine affects me that way. Do you two mind if I take a little nap?"

"Go right ahead, Aunt Jane. You know where my office is. There's an afghan you crocheted for me on the guest bed. Do you mind if Manny and I take a look at the scrapbook and the two cases we carted out with you and Mabel ... from the safe-room?"

"That's fine, dear. Here's the combination for both of them," she said, drawing a chain with a locket out from around her neck beneath her dress, and then up over her head. Patting the collar of her housedress back in place, she dropped the chain in Liz's hand. "I won't be long. Usually thirty minutes. Then I'm 'up and at'em' as my Morty would say. Maybe you two detective types can come up with some ideas on how I'm going to find my little treasures."

Chapter 13

Thursday, 7:30 p.m. – Day Two

A puff of air passed over the candle's flame. The flame flickered. Liz looked up at Manny. "Ghosts?"

"It's Morty," Manny whispered pulling his lips back from his teeth.

Liz smiled. "But, of course, my dear Watson," she said imitating Sherlock Holmes.

"Hey, I want to be Sherlock," Manny said.

"Nope. I thought of it first," Liz said grinning. "Kind of exciting, don't you think? Aunt Jane a millionaire."

"Maybe. Maybe more than one-mil from the sounds of it."

Manny leaned around the flickering candle, topped off their glasses with the last of the wine, and then grasped her fingers around her glass. "Are you thinking what I'm thinking?"

"Aunt Jane?"

"Yeah." Manny popped a cheese cube in his mouth, pushed the plate closer to Liz.

Liz lifted her gaze to Manny. "I'm worried about her ... not her precisely. She's spunky, smart, misses her husband. She isn't ready to crawl into a hole. She is ready to live it up. What I'm worried about is her safety."

His face mirrored her concern. "Let's have a look in those cases and that scrapbook. Maybe what she told us was a dream she's conjured up about her husband after he died. They were very close. Sometimes the remaining spouse, a soul-mate relationship, can play tricks on the memory." Manny retrieved the two cases he had put in the hallway. Both dogs lifted their heads, watched him leave the room, laid their heads back down when he returned.

"Great watch dogs we have under the table."

"Shh, Watson, they're eavesdropping. Specially-trained dogs."

Manny set the cases on the table beside the scrapbook and then crouched beside Liz, taking hold of her hands. "Whatever we find, I want you to know I'll help you with your aunt. She's a very sweet lady and obviously trusts you."

"She trusts you, too. She asked you to meet with her, and swore us both to keep what she said a secret." A wash of warmth slid through her body—the feeling of Manny's hands holding hers, so big, so strong. Something she had missed. Where had the time gone since she had broken off an engagement in college. A very wrong man. There had been one other, but she had turned away—several years ago. The way she had felt about them was vastly different than the trust, the warmth she felt when Manny quickly came to help her find her aunt. *I thought she might be dead.* Liz shuddered at the thought.

She picked up the scrapbook, drew back the cover revealing pages of Polaroid photos mounted with old-fashioned, black sticky corners to hold them in place. Manny looked over her shoulder as she turned the pages each holding two or three photos of her cherished little friends that had adorned her holiday tree.

"Look at that bracelet. I remember Uncle Morty wearing it."

"Okay, kiddo," Manny said giving her a quick peck on the cheek, "let's see what's in those cases."

"Very well, Watson." Liz grinned. "Are you ready to spin the combination?"

"Ready, Holmes."

Liz snapped on the kitchen lights, blew out the candle, and set it on the counter. Manny opened the locket removing the sliver of paper and handed it to Liz.

"She's numbered the cases. Do you see a number? Maybe by the handle?"

"Two ... pretty sure that's a two. Call out the code, Holmes. We're in this caper together," he said smiling.

Manny carefully advanced each tiny wheel to the position Liz called. With a click, he lifted the lid of the first case.

"This must be the one with the records or journals as she called them," Liz said picking up a CD in a clear plastic jewel case. "Look, there's a date, Uncle Morty's handwriting. It's the day he died. She must not have made any entries on the computer after that. It's as if time stopped for her that day."

"Not quite," Manny said. He had opened a savings account book, a register of transactions. She opened a savings account six months ago and made a deposit. It's the only entry."

"How much?" Liz asked leaning her head close to Manny's ear so she could see. "She deposited an even twelve thousand dollars."

"Nothing's wrong with your eyesight, Sherlock. I guess Jane was kidding about having a million," Manny said. "See this pink sticky note on the next page?"

Liz took the register so she could read what he was pointing to. "Looks like her username, password, and an answer to a security question: *What's your niece's name? Lizzy.* Sweet, huh?"

"Sweet, but not a good idea to keep the information with the register. Let's open the other case. Give me the code for number five," Manny said.

Liz called out the numbers. With a click, Manny lifted the lid.

Manny and Jane looked at each other amazed at what lay on the table in front of them.

Gleaming in the light of the overhead white globe inside a green tiffany shade was a rectangular container packed neatly with gold coins and a small plastic zip-bag containing what Jane had called her gemstones. The stones glittered through the clear plastic—red, yellow, but mostly clear diamonds.

"Has to be a few thousand with the coins alone," Manny whispered.

"Has to be," Liz whispered.

They both looked up as Jane ambled back into the kitchen. She stepped to the table, touched the CD and the folder containing the bank register. Turning her eyes to the other open case, she ran her fingers over the container of gold coins her lips curving up. She sat down, hands in her lap. "Well?"

Manny shut the case. "Ladies, we have work to do. Liz, can you put on a pot of coffee?"

"You bet, Watson."

Jane looked at Lizzy questioning.

"Inside joke," Liz said kissing her aunt on the cheek. "Aunt Jane, there are a couple of yellow legal pads on my desk. Can you get them

… and pens. Grab one for yourself, too. There are more in the center drawer. We have to make a list of what you called your treasures, and their descriptions. Tomorrow you and mom can make up a list of everything else that you lost—clothes, furniture, whatever for the insurance claim. Tonight, we plan on how we're going to find the big stuff … dare I say gold, diamonds, and the rest of your Apple Computer stock. And, how about some dinner with our coffee?" Liz asked her hand on the freezer compartment of her refrigerator.

"Only if it's easy," Manny said.

"Watson, I don't cook. Everything is easy." She pulled out three packages of frozen Lean Cuisine glazed chicken with rice, and green beans and popped them in the microwave.

With the scrapbook as a guide, Liz made a list of the photos as Manny turned the pages, and Jane added the descriptions including the gems she had meticulously glued on her little holiday tree friends. She lovingly put her hand on the photo of the angel and described how she had adhered Morty's gold wedding band over the angel's head.

"You can see how thick his ring was, Lizzy," she said. Grabbing Manny's hand from the scrapbook, she held up his thumb. "Morty's ring finger was bigger than Manny's thumb," Jane said.

"With the size of the ring and the thickness of the band, I would imagine it'd bring a pretty penny at today's gold prices," Manny said. "Then, you factor in the diamonds …" Manny shook his head.

"Oh, yes," Jane said. "Over three-thousand dollars as I recall. Of course, the actual price is in one of the journal files."

Liz looked at her aunt. Nothing she said fazed her anymore. "All right, that's the last photo," Liz said. "Any ideas on how we're going to retrieve the holiday tree items, not to mention the cases? I have a couple of easy ones to start with."

"Go ahead. I'm for starting with easy," Manny said grinning.

"Well, with these photos, I thought we might run an ad in the paper, Lost and Found section. Maybe we could get the editor to do a human-interest story on Aunt Jane and her holiday tree. We won't mention the gems in the description. Maybe whoever finds one of her friends will think the diamonds are fake."

"And, if we get any calls, I'll start mapping where the items are found. Maybe we'll see a pattern. Trouble is the telephone. What telephone number do you want to give out? Jane, while you were taking your nap we talked about … well, we're concerned about your safety."

"Good heavens, why?"

"When it comes to stock certificates, we have to be very careful what information we let out. If it leaks that you have more than one case missing, some culprit could get the idea of blackmailing you."

"Oh, I see what you mean, but—"

"How about we use my cell number," Liz said. "I carry it all the time. I could even pretend I was Aunt Jane."

"Nice try, Stitch—"

Manny stopped seeing the grin on Liz's face. "What?"

"You called me Stitch when we first met … that murder case—"

"Oh, yeah, I forgot. As I was saying before I was interrupted by that silly grin on your face … Stitch … if the newspaper does a human interest story on Jane, the local television channel will pick it up and your voice, which sounds like a kid, won't match your Aunt beaming into the camera."

"My voice does not sound like a kid," Liz said arching her brows.

"No, but you get what I mean."

"I do," Liz chuckled. "But so what?"

"So, same as Jane. You'd be making yourself known. That would not be a good thing … for either of you."

"I'll get another cell just for … Jane's Business. Never identify myself. Ask questions. See if the caller is legit. Set up a meeting—"

"A meeting with both of us, like in you and me," Manny said punctuating the words you and me. "Jane waits while we—"

"Do you're detective work," Jane cut in. "Oh, I like this."

Liz and Manny looked at Jane. "Aunt Jane, if a bad guy finds something, it could be dangerous."

"Speaking of dangerous, you haven't told us what's in the other four cases … except for some stock certificates. How many shares are out there and what else is in the cases?" Manny asked.

"Well," Jane pulled her yellow pad in front of her and began writing. "There. I think that's about it," Jane said turning the pad to Liz. Manny put his hands on her shoulders, looking over her head he read along with her.

<u>Case 1</u>
Four account books.
Two gold bars, approximate total a little more than one-hundred thousand.

Case 4
Twenty gold bars. Each bar is one kilo, total value over one million.

Case 3
Stock certificates and four gold bars. Total value approximately a quarter of a million.

Case 6
Twenty gold bars. Total value over one million.

Case 2 – from safe-room
Journals and savings register

Case 5– from safe-room
Diamonds, and gold coins (about $5,000).

Sighing at the same time, they both closed their eyes. Manny moved first.

"Stitch, got anything stronger than coffee?"

"Beer?"

"It'll do."

Liz stepped quickly to the refrigerator, grabbed a bottle of beer, looked around at her aunt, and grabbed two more bottles. She handed the bottles to Manny to twist off the caps.

Liz tapped her pen on the yellow pad. "Okay, how about we put an ad in the newspaper featuring the angel and—"

"I know. I know," Jane said waving her hand like a school girl trying to get the attention of her teacher. "Eggbert."

"Okay, but any particular reason?" Liz asked writing Eggbert on the pad.

"Yes, he holds a very valuable yellow diamond in his tummy. I didn't know what to do with the stone—it was so large. And then one evening, sipping my wine, I looked at my tree and saw Eggbert smiling at me. 'You're perfect' I told him."

"How much is this yellow diamond worth?" Manny asked.

"Over a hundred thousand."

"Dollars?" Manny closed his eyes waiting for her answer. Given what he'd seen on her yellow pad with the list of the cases and their contents, he knew she was going to say, yes.

"Of course, dollars, silly. What did you think, Euros?"

"No, no. I was afraid you meant dollars, Jane."

"It's a perfect, flawless, seven-carat stone, radiant cut," Jane said gazing at the ceiling, picturing the stone in her mind's eye.

Liz sucked in a big breath and then added to their plan. "What do you think about listing both the angel and Eggbert on EBay. And, Amazon is selling things now just like EBay."

"I like the online idea—no direct contact," Manny said. "But if you get the ad in tomorrow so it can run on Monday, let's see if anyone responds. If not, then online. Also, I'll start checking the local pawn shops. If we can establish a pattern, a trail where things are found, then I'll expand the search. The storm turned north, up the coast. Didn't hit south of Volusia County."

"Manny, the News Journal ad will include the cell number. I'll pick up a new cell at Wal-Mart in the morning."

"Okay, but don't give out too much information over the phone. AND, promise me you'll let me know if you get a call."

"Wait," Jane put both palms up. "I've told you this much, I guess I'd better tell you the rest—my bank accounts."

Jane picked up the savings account register and then set it back on the table. "No, I'm talking about case 1, the first on the list."

"Oh, I thought you meant more account journals," Liz said.

"No, no. I never took the time ... you see we sold all but three-hundred shares of the stock just before Morty died. I already told you about those remaining certificates. The total value had grown so large that at the time of the sale we instructed our Fidelity Investment representative to transfer all the proceeds into our account."

"And, is that what happened?" Liz asked.

"Yes. Morty was then going to transfer it into various CD's ... but ... but he died before any transfers were made."

"Jane, the entry in your savings register is six months ago. Are—"

"Are you telling us there's more?" *Please, God, not more,* Liz thought.

"Yes. There are four accounts. Each has a balance of around a million—give or take a thousand."

Chapter 14

Thursday, 10:00 p.m. – Day Two

It was late.

Jane took Liz up on her offer to spend the night. After a hug from both of her detectives, she wearily shuffled down the hall to the bedroom, the cozy room Liz used as an office but switchable for the occasional guest—flowered chintz curtains framing the window and a matching bedspread. So unlike the austere appearance her niece had assumed—always dressed in black. The only relief a white top, with or without sleeves, sporty or sometimes silky.

Manny's gaze followed Jane out of the kitchen and then turned to Liz.

"I'd better be going," he said rising to leave. "What do you want to do with these cases?"

"Under the mattress!"

"But of course, Sherlock. A most acceptable place. A bit lumpy but a small inconvenience for dear Aunt Jane," he said chuckling as he stepped into the front hall.

"Happy you agree, Holmes."

"And?" Manny leaned against the wall.

Liz leaned against the opposite wall, arms hanging at her side. "First, she has to go to the bank and change the account numbers. Like waiting at the front door when they open. After tending to the accounts,

I think she should open a safe-deposit box for the gold coins and the diamonds in the case."

"Sounds right. I hope she goes along with you."

Liz followed him to the door. He reached for the door knob, turned wrapping his arms around her, holding her against him for a brief second. He quickly kissed her leaving her wide-eyed in surprise.

Peaches squirted passed him, scampered around the bushes in the yard then jumped into the car beside her master.

Liz, arms hugging her body, holding tight the feeling of Manny's kiss, watched the man with his dog drive down the street until the car's taillights disappeared. Letting Maggie in for the night, she shut the door, leaned against it, closing her eyes.

"What a day," she whispered.

Driving the short distance to his houseboat, Manny mulled over the evening.

Stitch!

She looked so darned cute in those black Capri's and jeweled sandals. Sherlock—smart but vulnerable. Shocked at the revelation of her aunt's mysterious life. We were both caught up in the fantasy of it.

Manny's wife, Marie, had died over five years ago. The sudden desire for Liz tonight was different than anything he had felt before. His need to hold her, kiss her had overcome his usually cool, tempered urges. *She must be five years younger than me,* he thought. *So vivacious, fun, easy to be with. And, she certainly understands my job. She's worked hard to become a private investigator. I know what that's like.*

He pulled into his driveway, leaned over and opened the door for Peaches to perform her nightly routine. He opened his door, his leg dropped outside the car, but he didn't move the rest of his body. He continued to sit in the car, looking out over the river, troubled feelings seeping through his body.

There's too much money at stake. Jane's definitely in danger. So is Liz. She's so darn independent ... and beautiful.

Manny climbed out of the car as a cloud skittered away from the moon, leaving its light shining through the trees, shining down on the empty space where a house had stood until it was destroyed by a fire. Burned to the ground. Because of that fire he bought the property at way below market value, otherwise he would never have been able to afford it.

He shook his head free of an image that had begun popping into his head every time he saw Liz.

An image of a house.

No, a home.

"You're moving too fast, Salinas. Get a grip. Come on, Peaches, let's hit the sack."

Chapter 15

Friday, 8:30 a.m. – Day Three

The morning sun streamed through the double-hung kitchen window, four over four panes, adding to the cozy sunny-yellow walls and warm pine cabinets. A day in paradise? Hardly.

Tension filled the air as Jane fumbled with the kitchen wall phone. She was hoping to speak with the bank manager, hoping the manager came in early, hoping to put an immediate freeze on her accounts.

Liz, already dressed for action, sat drafting an ad for the newspaper shaking her foot to the tune of the percolating coffee. She looked up hearing her aunt drop the receiver, the curly wire stretching as the phone bounced off the floor.

Jane muttered, picked up the receiver, and punched in the numbers. She didn't know the manager's name. Rarely went to the bank preferring to do everything online and direct deposit. She got what little cash she needed at the end of her transactions at the grocery store.

Fidgeting with the cord, she counted the rings. An automated voice came on the line stating the bank wasn't open but—the recorded voice was interrupted.

"This is Ann. Can I help you?"

"Yes, Ann, this is Jane Haliday."

"Hi, Mrs. Haliday. I'm glad you called. Are you ready to do something with those accounts? You really must move your money into different instruments to protect—"

"Ann, my house was destroyed by that twister. I presume you heard about it?"

"Oh, my God, that's awful. Are you all right?"

"Yes, that is I wasn't hurt. My Mortimer insisted that we install a safe-room but everything else on my block is gone. It's all gone, Ann."

Liz quickly went to her aunt's side pulling a chair up for her to sit on, kneeling beside her, patting her hand as tears began to cascade down her red face. Liz handed her a tissue. Jane blew her nose and stuffed the tissue in the housedress she wore last night.

"Excuse me, Ann, not quite myself. I'm afraid I've done a very stupid thing. Oh, Morty must be so upset with me." Jane looked up, closed her eyes then looked at Liz who nodded for her to continue.

"Ann, please put a freeze on all of my accounts. I'll drive right over to find out what I should do."

"Certainly. Hang on a minute while I pull your records up on the computer."

Jane heard the clickity-click of Ann's keyboard, and then an audible gasp.

"Mrs. Haliday, are you still there?"

"Yes, I'm here."

"Mrs. Haliday, your accounts show a zero balance. The funds were withdrawn yesterday morning. Hold on. Betty Tisdale, our manager, just came in. Something's wrong here. I have to put you on hold, Mrs. Haliday. I'll be right back."

"Lizzy, my accounts are empty. Someone must have found the case with the account registers and the codes. Stupid. Stupid. Stupid." Trembling, Jane's head sank, her hand on her cheek, her elbow on her knee.

"Mrs. Haliday, This is Betty Tisdale. Thank goodness you called. I've been trying to reach you ... several times yesterday. There was no answer. Left messages, even drove to your house but, as you told Ann, I saw that your park was hit by that twister. Mrs. Haliday, the bank is set up to trigger an automatic alert when large sums of money are transferred out of an account. Did you transfer this money?"

"No, Ms. Tisdale," Jane whispered. "What should I do?"

"Oh, dear, dear. Please, come in as soon as you can. I'll make sure the doors are open. Ask for me. In the meantime, I'll start a trace. But the thing is, Mrs. Haliday, whoever withdrew the money must have had the account numbers, codes, answers to the security questions. If you didn't initiate the transfers it must have been a hacker. Can you come in now?"

Placing the two steel briefcases on the floor of Jane's car, Liz hugged her aunt, wished her luck, and asked again if Jane wanted her to go with her. Jane said she could handle it for now and drove off to the bank, and Liz drove in the direction of Wal-Mart to pick up another cell phone. Her next stop was at the News Journal to drop off the ad looking for the angel, Eggbert, and a steel briefcase.

Sleep had eluded Liz—between all the puzzle pieces that her aunt kept dropping into her story, and trying to figure out how she was going to help her aunt retrieve not only her millions but the gold and her holiday tree friends, and then there was Manny's kiss.

Liz kept glancing in her rearview mirror to see if she looked different. She certainly felt different. How could one kiss set her heart thumping, her face to flush, saying nothing about wanting to pick up the phone to hear his voice.

The night wasn't a total loss. She agreed with Manny that her aunt, and by extension herself, were heading into something that could be dangerous. On the other hand ... no, there was no other hand. Jane's bank accounts were drained. On one of her trips to the kitchen during the night for a mug of warm milk, Liz began formulating a plan.

She was going undercover.

Oh, not disappearing in body.

A virtual disappearance.

Her errands accomplished, Liz pulled into a strip mall and parked in front of a hair salon. One of her clients had mentioned awhile back, that the owner was particularly good. Exceptionally good with color.

Johnny Cash was singing a *Man Named Sue* when Liz stepped into the small shop. *Well, I'm going that far,* she thought.

A well-groomed blonde put down a razor, told her patron she'd be right back, and walked up to greet Liz.

"Can I help you?" she asked.

"Yes, are you the owner? Mildred?"

"I surely am, hon, but I go by Milly."

"I was told to ask for you. Would you have time to do a color? Blonde?"

Milly looked at the woman's reddish-brown hair. "Give me five, hon, and I'll be right with you. Have a seat. I won't be long." Milly bent over the appointment book. "What's your name?"

"Elizabeth, Elizabeth Stevens."

"OK, Elizabeth," Milly said flashing a smile. She hustled back to her booth to finish shaving the neck of a gray-haired woman.

Chapter 16

Friday, 9:00 a.m. – Day Three

The humidity was oppressive as the sun continued to rise in the sky. Manny threw his legs over the side of the bed, stood, shook his hands, performed a few knee bends, and let Peaches out. Friday. He was late. Really late. He couldn't sleep. At 4:00 a.m. he dozed off, but he knew he wasn't ready to do the people's business.

Peaches was barking for him to come out, so he quickly pulled on his jogging gear. They began at a moderate pace. Manny didn't feel like burning up the pavement this morning. He continually twisted around to see if Liz was out on the road. Of course, she wasn't. He was too late. He seemed to be looking for her a lot these days. She was constantly creeping into his thoughts, tugging at his heart.

The ring of his cell pulled him back from the images flying around in his head, to the road in front of him, and the slap of his feet on the asphalt. Turning down his driveway he pulled out his cell. An officer was calling.

"Yeah?"

"One of our patrol cars found a dead guy behind a dumpster in an alley. Looks like an overdose. Given the renewed spotlight on drugs around here, thought you might want to swing by the scene or do you want us to transport him to the morgue?"

"Transport. I'll meet you there in thirty."

Manny put on his dark glasses as he turned east into the sun. At the morgue he parked behind his officer's squad car. The two men who had processed the scene met him at the door and began their report.

There didn't seem to be any foul play. They were on a routine patrol when they spotted the guy's foot sticking out from behind the dumpster. They thought he was asleep but found his sleep was permanent. They had seen the guy around. He lived on the street. A known addict with a line of marks on his arm to prove it. No ID on his body. They knew him as Hector, the street guy. The only thing in his pocket was a business card from a local pawn shop which they gave to Manny. They figured Hector had been dead a day, probably longer.

The medical examiner escorted Manny to the refrigerated vault, pulled out the drawer and unzipped the body bag. Manny checked the corpse for any sign of a struggle and snapped a couple of pictures of the man with his cell. He thanked the ME and caught up with his officers in the parking lot. He told them that he was going to the department but would stop at the pawn shop on the business card later in the day.

At noon, having finished writing up two reports, Manny stood, slapped his thigh, and Peaches' wet nose nudged his hand. The pair left the building and climbed into the captain's plain black SUV after Peaches had a quick romp on the grass chasing a squirrel that scampered up at a tree, sat on a branch and looked down. Manny could have sworn the critter stuck his tongue out at his dog.

Smiling, Manny drove in the direction of Sammy's Pawn Shop, the shop printed on the business card found on the dead guy.

Stopping at a light, his thoughts turned to Jane. He wondered how she made out at the bank. Then Liz filled his mind and a sudden ache to hold her swamped his body.

"Peaches, this woman is getting out of hand," he said flipping open his cell. Peaches slurped his ear and then returned to her post at the window.

Liz picked up on the first ring.

"Hang up. I'll call you right back on my new cell. Jane's Business phone. You can store the number."

The line went dead.

She hadn't given him a chance to say a word.

He closed his cell which instantly rang in his hand.

"Hi," she whispered.

"Why are you whispering? You sound different," he whispered back. "Now you've got me whispering."

"I am different. My name is Elizabeth Stevens. Still ES. Nice, huh?"

"What happened to Sherlock?"

"Gone. I heard blondes have more fun," she giggled. "I'm under cover when talking on this phone," she said continuing to speak in a hushed voice.

Manny rolled his eyes as he turned into a parking spot in front of the pawn shop. "What's this about blondes?"

"Later."

"Your aunt. What happened at the bank?"

"Cleaned out. Four mil gone. Early Thursday. Must have found the case either the night of the twister or sometime in the morning ... Thursday. I just walked into my office. Where are you?"

"Sammy's Pawn Shop. Police business, but I'll check if anyone pawned something of Jane's. I'll call you if I come up with anything." He paused. "Blonde, huh? Sounds like fun." He chuckled as they both disconnected.

It was almost one-thirty when Manny strode into the pawn shop. A sixty something man asked how he could help the captain.

"Not sure. Are you the manager?"

"I'm Sammy. This is my shop. What can I do for you, officer?"

"I found one of your business cards in the pocket of a man who appeared to have overdosed. In that he had your card, I was wondering if he had been in recently. Maybe pawned something for a fix."

Manny pulled out his cell, advanced to Hector's picture and showed it to Sammy.

"Ohhh, too bad. It's Hector." The owner looked up at Manny and then back at the picture. "He and I do a lot of business. I'm not surprised. Overdose, you say?"

"Appears that way," Manny replied.

"He was in here a couple of days ago. Late. I was closing. Brought in a bracelet. A beauty. I asked him where he got it and he gave me a cockamamie story about finding it."

"Can I see it?"

"Sure, it's right—"

The man looked in the case, in the next case ... "That's strange. I could swear it was here. Let me check my merchandise log. Maybe someone bought … yes, well, he picked it up Thursday. Yesterday." The man looked up at Manny, raised brows. "When did you find him? This morning? Because, it says here he retrieved it after my assistant opened Thursday."

"Hmm. We think he's been dead a day, maybe longer. The medical examiner hasn't had time to establish time of death. Who bought the bracelet?"

"Hector did. At least that's what the slip says. Turned in the pawn ticket. See. Here's the ticket."

"Can you describe the bracelet?" Manny asked.

"As I said it was a beauty. Solid gold, large links encrusted with diamonds. I'm afraid I wasn't honest with Hector. I didn't let him know how much it was worth. Thought he'd just blow the money on drugs. Gave him fifteen dollars. He didn't know the value—finding it and all. He was very happy with fifteen. You don't suppose he stole it?"

"Hold on a minute. I have to make a call." Manny tapped in Liz's phone.

Hearing her pick up, he said, "Hi, it's Manny."

"I know, silly. What's up?"

"Can you send a picture of Morty's bracelet to my cell? The one Jane had in the scrapbook?"

"No problem. I have the scrapbook right here, so I can take a picture of the picture … I heard that chuckle. Here it is. I'm disconnecting. I'll send it from Jane's business cell. I heard that again. What's with all these chuckles?"

Liz disconnected his call leaving a smile on Manny's face.

His phone chirped and he pulled up the picture of Morty's bracelet.

"Is this the bracelet?" Manny asked showing Sammy the picture Liz had sent.

"Why, yes. Do you know where it came from?"

"It's a long story, but the condensed version is that the twister that tore through that Port Orange—"

"I read about that. Terrible. A couple of people lost their lives I believe."

"That's it. This bracelet was picked up by that twister. So, it's possible Hector did find it. Found it where the twister dropped it. But, now the question is, who turned in the pawn ticket Thursday morning? Hector was dead?"

Chapter 17

Friday, 2:00 p.m. – Day Three

The chainsaw reverberated against the little frame house as the blades sliced through section after section of the fallen branch that blocked the driveway.

Watching her daddy from the kitchen window, Bella saw him lugging pieces of the limb to the curb for pickup while the neighbor, who brought his saw, continued to hold the blade against the wood as well as knifing through small offshoots. After the last cut, the man strolled on down the street, waving goodbye to the little girl in the window.

Donald wiped his brow with the back of his hand. He smiled at his daughter sitting in her highchair. He had pulled the chair up to the window so she could see what was causing the noise. He walked up the wheelchair ramp and through the back door into the kitchen.

"OK, kiddo, let me take a shower and then I'll put you in the car. Time to check on that rock that was giving Eggbert a bellyache."

Dressed in a fresh pair of jeans and T-shirt, Donald stopped into Bella's room for her white floppy hat and a pair of yellow socks to go with her red and white playsuit he had dressed her in earlier. Putting the hat on her head and socks on her feet Bella raised her arms to her daddy ready to be picked up.

"Eggbert, Daddy. He has to go with us."

"Right." Donald reached down for the little guy and put him under Bella's arm.

Settling Bella on the back seat, buckling the seatbelt, he gave her cheek a peck and walked around to the other side of the car sliding in behind the wheel. He sighed as he turned the key in the ignition. At least the car started, that was a blessing.

"Don't worry, Daddy. Eggbert's tummy doesn't hurt anymore." Bella held her friend up to the window so he could watch with her as they passed houses, palm trees, and little shops.

"That's good, sweetie. We'll find out what kind of a rock Eggbert was hiding in that tummy of his."

Donald parked in front of the small jewelry shop, wrestled Bella's wheelchair out of the back, and transferred his little girl into the chair. Entering the shop, a gentleman in a brown suit and tie behind the counter, looked up.

"Well, hello there, young lady. How are you today?"

"Fine thank you and Eggbert is fine, too."

"What can I do for you, sir?"

"I have this stone," Donald said, fishing in his jean's pocket. Unwrapping the tissue, he set it on the glass counter in front of the man. "I was hoping you could tell me what it is."

"Let's have a look. Certainly sparkles," he said picking up the jeweler's loupe hanging from a chain around his neck. He secured the loupe in his eye socket.

"Mister, what's that?" Bella asked.

"It's my loupe, a magnifying glass," he said as he examined the stone. "Here, look through the glass at your doll's foot."

"Oooh, his foot is big."

The man smiled, secured the loupe again in his eye, and picked up the stone.

"This is quite a stone, Mr.?" he looked up at Donald.

"Donald Sanderson, and this is Bella."

Bella smiled up at the nice man, holding Eggbert tight in her lap.

The man let the loupe drop to his shirt. "Yes, sir, quite a stone. Where did it come from? Family heirloom?"

"You wouldn't believe me if I told you," Donald chuckled, looking down at Bella. "You might say it has become a family heirloom. What is it?"

"It's a very beautiful, yellow diamond. Almost seven carats, radiant cut. Flawless."

"Wow, Bella. That means our new heirloom is very precious." Donald stared up at the man staring at him.

"How much is it worth?"

"Well," the man shook his head. Sighed. "It would retail for around a hundred-twenty-thousand."

"Dollars?"

"Do you have insurance, Mr. Sanderson?"

... Donald continued to stare at the man, slack jawed.

"Mr. Sanderson, do you have insurance on this beautiful diamond? You really should—"

"No ... no. No insurance."

"Well, I suggest you take out a policy right away," the man said picking up a black-velvet bag. "Let me give you this pouch, help protect it. I thank you for showing this diamond to me. I have never seen one of this brilliance, this size." He handed the velvet pouch to Donald and smiled down at Bella.

Bella tugged on her daddy's jeans. "Eggbert wants to go home, Daddy. He's hungry."

Chapter 18

Friday, 5:30 p.m. – Day Three

She was to bring her bright, sunny disposition to dinner—the family needed her charm and wit even if she faked it.

Liz looked in her rearview mirror, adjusting one of the blond curls. *Well if this doesn't bring a few laughs, then they all need to go to the psych ward.*

"Yoo-hoo. Anybody home?" Liz called out letting Maggie scoot in the house in front of her.

"We're in the kitchen, Liz," Martha replied. "Your father's pouring the wine."

"Hello, everyone." Liz stood in the doorway with her brightest, broadest, beaming smile.

"Good heavens. You're a blonde." Martha jumped up from her chair. "Let me look at you. Turn around."

"What do you think, Dad?" Liz asked, prancing across the red-brick linoleum to plant a kiss on his cheek.

"Well, I like it, I guess. You know that nothing you do surprises me anymore—bright red kinky curls as a child, then dark red, then, what do you call it, ironed?"

"Straightened is the word, Dad. Not ironed. And, what does my favorite aunt think?"

"Lizzy, I'm your only aunt, and I love it."

The stove's timer buzzed and the conversation instantly switched to the baked lasagna Martha pulled out of the oven. Liz had done what she was asked to do—switched gloom and doom from the twister to animated, happy chatter.

After dinner, the dishes washed and put away, and a last cup of decaf coffee, Harry walked his daughter to her car, a frown on his face.

"Lizzy, is something going on with your business?"

"Well, yes and no. I wish there was more of it," she chuckled. "Why do you ask?"

"It's the hair thing. Not that you can't be a blonde ... you'd be beautiful if it was pink like Jane's, but—"

"Dad, put your security guard alert away. Everything is fine."

"OK. I just wondered. How do you think Jane's doing? She seems to be worried about her finances."

"She's doing ... okay. I mean ... it's a terrible ordeal."

"Well, you're close to her. If you find out she needs money, please let your mom and I know. We can help her out a little. I thought Morty had set things up for a nice retirement. But then his dying so suddenly—"

"Dad, don't worry. Uncle Morty definitely, well, he tried to set things up for a nice retirement. She's still dealing with the shock of it all."

Chapter 19

Saturday, 7:05 a.m. – Day Four

A low weather system drifted down from Georgia during the night bringing cooler dry air. The day's forecast: a high of eighty-nine degrees and clear blue skies. A brisk breeze swept ashore off the Atlantic Ocean but Kathleen didn't notice. Her brown hair poking through her billed cap in a ponytail, she inhaled the salty air as she gazed at the sparkling water lapping the shore. After a week on the job designing websites, her anticipation accelerated as she donned her bright red jogging shorts, white tank top, and sneakers.

Ahh. Saturday.

She stretched her legs pulling her foot up behind her—first the right then the left. A few head rolls and she was ready. Smiling, she jogged down the path leading to the beach. Twisting her head—shoulder to shoulder—something caught her eye off to the side where the sand met the marshy grass. She squinted as she closed the distance to the object.

At the same time a man with tousled black hair jogged toward her in tan running shorts, also turned his head toward the object.

Something caught the sun's rays.

The two joggers collided.

He knocked Kathleen off her feet.

"Oh, I'm so sorry. Here, let me help you up," the man said extending his hand. Kathleen grasped his fingers, laughing, her green eyes sparkling in the sunshine.

"It was my fault," she said brushing the sand from the seat of her shorts. "I saw ... there ... on that bush," she said pointing to her right.

"I saw it, too. Turned my head. Again, I'm sorry."

They stood smiling at each other, both reaching for the object at the same time. This time, however, the man lost his footing. Kathleen, her arm stretching out to grasp the object, didn't notice.

"It's a little pig," she said turning it over in her fingers. She looked up at the man, then down. He was on the ground smiling up at her.

"Oh, my gosh, here," she said extending one hand, holding the pig out in the other. "See, isn't it cute?"

"Very cute." The man let go of her hand. "Being as we're knocking each other around, my name's Patrick."

"I'm Kathleen. Are you okay?"

"Only my pride that a whippet of a girl could so easily knock me over. Kathleen, eh. From Ireland by any chance?"

"My dad's Irish. You?"

"Mom was a Coleen. I thought I detected a slight brogue. Let me take a look at that pig," he said grinning. "Light. Looks like an ornament you might set on a Christmas tree. No string on top, though."

Kathleen carefully took the ornament from Patrick's hand. "You're right. It's glass. I wonder how it got here ... without breaking?"

"Well, I think we should talk about joint custody over a cup of coffee, unless—"

"Coffee sounds great. I headed out this morning without my usual cup of caffeine. There's a little café, quarter mile, you up to it?"

"Sure."

The pair jogged easily side by side up the path then down the edge of the road.

"You know, if we're going to have joint custody of Miss Piggy, I think we should set a date."

"A date?" Kathleen looked up at Patrick matching his stride. He was a head taller than she, had a runner's body like hers, and a devilish grin.

"Yes. We haven't known each other long, and I don't usually go around suggesting a date to be married ... unless you're already married," he said.

There was that devilish grin again. "No, heavens no. Not married. But I can see what you mean about Miss Piggy. Maybe joint custody to begin with, but she certainly would not want to be bandied about between two homes after what she's been through. After all, she survived what must have been a harrowing experience to bring her to a crash landing in the grassy dunes along Route A1A," Kathleen said making a serious face, brows scrunched together, lips tight.

"Hey, she didn't crash land. There's not a mark on her," Patrick said. "So about that date? I like September."

"Umm. I've always thought I'd like a September wedding."

"Come on. Really?"

"Really. But can't do it this September. Big graphic's conference in California. No time to plan a wedding."

"Well then, next September."

Kathleen held the ornament out in front of her. "What do you think, Miss Piggy?"

"It's okay with me," Kathleen said mimicking a high squeaky voice.

Patrick held the café door open for Kathleen, guided her to a booth, and she carefully set Miss Piggy on the table between them.

"Now, who gets her first?" Patrick asked.

"Do you always grin like that?" Kathleen asked. "It's like you've got a tickle up your sleeve."

Chapter 20

Saturday, 9:35 a.m. – Day Four

Drought conditions in Volusia County had eased as a result of the downpours that followed in the wake of the twister. Two miles northeast of Happy Days Estates was another small park of manufactured homes. Canals and ponds in the park had risen almost a foot as a result of Wednesday's storm.

Two little boys, seven year olds, splashed in the pond hidden by bushes and old arching oak trees, Spanish moss dangling from the branches brushed the water. Billy Clark's mom, Sally, had forbidden him to play or swim in the murky water believing it was infested with all sorts of creatures. An alligator had been captured and carted off several years back. Same was the rule laid down by Min Chong for his son Ricky.

But heck, it was summer, and the boys thought a quick dip, very quick, couldn't hurt. They would keep an eye peeled for any log that moved. Billy, a towhead, had heard his mother say that gators often floated in the water, only their craggy hide showing. A craggy hide resembling a log that could snatch a little boy in its teeth and swallow him whole.

"Ricky, look over there," Billy screamed.

"Where?"

"There. There. That log. It moved," Billy screamed again pointing to the other side of the pond.

Ricky grabbed a stick floating near him. He threw it at the log-like thing. His toss didn't quite reach the log-like thing, but it came close. The log-like thing didn't move, or more important, didn't open its mouth.

"You're a scaredy cat, Billy. That's just a big, old, dead branch."

"I'm going home," Billy said. He pulled on a bush to help him climb up out of the pond. He lost his footing slipping backward. "Oooh, I stepped on a dead fish," he squealed peering down into the murky water.

Ricky waded up beside Billy. "Let me see. Move." Ricky pushed his friend out of the way so he could see the dead fish.

"Sure is shiny, Billy." He touched the fish with his toe. "That's not a dead fish, stupid. It's a metal box. Hold my shirt in case I fall."

Ricky reached down, his head submerging under the water. Tugging, he pulled the object from its shallow grave. Billy laughed at him.

"What's so funny," Ricky asked his head popping out of the water, his long black hair sticking to his cheeks and neck. His hand swiped the muck off his face.

"There's some of that moss stuff hanging down your back. You look like a girl with a ponytail."

"Shut up. I don't look like any old girl. Pull it off."

Billy reached for the glob of moss but slipped, his whole body going under the water. He emerged sputtering. "Ricky, there's another box. I slipped on it. Wait. You hold my shirt this time. If I don't come back up in two minutes pull me up so I don't drown."

"You're so dumb. Two minutes you'd be dead," Ricky said smirking.

Ricky gripped Billy's shirt as he disappeared under the water. Billy quickly popped to the surface, a smile on his face and the handle of another box in his hand.

Laughing, the boys struggled up the bank each gripping a shiny case. Gasping for air they laid on the grass, holding the handles of the cases by their sides. Billy rolled his head looking at his buddy. "We found sunken treasure, Ricky. Some pirate lost it. His ship came up the canal long, long ago. His body's probably rotting down there."

The boys shimmied farther away from the edge of the pond. Their shorts and T-shirts dripping wet from their adventure in the pirate's pond.

"I'm going home," Billy said bug-eyed as he looked at the pond for the pirate. "My mom said she wasn't going to be gone very long."

"Yeah, me, too," Ricky said, reaching for his shoes.

Both boys pulled on their sneakers, slapped the nylon-flaps tight, and with cases in hand scampered down the street.

Billy peeled off first and then Ricky four houses down. They didn't wave, or say goodbye to each other, as they ran into the safety of their houses away from alligators and pirates.

Billy rushed in the backdoor as his mother was putting a jug of milk into the refrigerator. She glanced over at her little boy as he shut the door, leaned back against it gulping for air.

"What's that you have there, young man? Your shirt's wet. Have you been in that pond? I told you—"

"Ricky and I—"

"I might have known you were with Ricky. You two always manage to get into trouble when you're together. Now let me see that briefcase."

"We were just sitting on the edge, honest, Mom, dangling our feet, splashing. We saw this shiny thing and when I reached for it I slipped part way into the water."

"Part way? Looks like all the way to me," his mom said taking the case from her son's outstretched hand. "Certainly is muddy. Combination lock." She shook the case. "I don't hear anything. Must be empty. Maybe not. Water could have gotten inside. Well, we can't open it so put it in the garage. I'll put it out for the garbage man next week. Then, you get into the shower. No telling what you were exposed to in that water."

Ricky ran down the street dragging the suitcase by the handle. It was too heavy for him to carry like Billy did with his case. He banged through the back door and smack into his father walking to the kitchen table, newspaper in one hand and a cup of coffee in the other.

"Richard, where have you been?" he asked wiping coffee off his shirt. I come home from picking up a newspaper and you're not here." He looked at his son. "You're filthy. Is that moss in your hair? You've been in that pond again haven't you? March straight to your room, mister, change your clothes, and then outside to finish the weeding."

Ricky hesitated a moment, his adventure getting the better of him. "Look what I found, Father," Ricky said pushing his prize on the floor to his father's feet. "I took a little break from the weeding when Billy came over. He begged me to go to the pond with him. I found this on the edge. Billy found one too."

"That's it. No more playing with Billy unless you've finished your chores," his father said yanking the case to the side. He was startled at how heavy it was. "Now, go do as I say."

Min Chong lugged the case to the sink and wiped it off. He stared at the combination lock. *So heavy ... maybe tools.*

Having changed into a pair of dry shorts, Ricky tiptoed quietly by his father hoping he could get out of the house before he received a swat on his bottom for disobeying him. But, no such luck. His father saw him.

"Richard, you said that Billy found a case. Is it like this one?"

"Yes, sir."

"Here's a dollar. Go ask Billy if you can buy it if he doesn't want to keep it."

"Should I do the weeding first?"

"No, you can finish your job when you get back. But, no going to the pond. Remember you're a piece of mosquito candy. I see a couple bites on your neck," Min said giving a friendly squeeze to his son's shoulder.

Chapter 21

Saturday, 10:08 a.m. – Day Four

Ricky was proud of himself. He didn't give Billy the dollar bill because his mom told him to put it in the garbage. But, Ricky didn't tell his father he had the dollar in his pocket as he banged in the backdoor, Billy's case hitting the door frame as it swung through.

Min took the case and told his son to get busy with the weeding. His eyes followed the boy out the door. He didn't know how to be a father, and certainly not a father and a mother. He hated himself when he yelled at Richard.

Min Chong was the son of South Korean immigrants, an educated couple who played in the Seoul Philharmonic Orchestra—his mother the violin, his father the French horn. Because of the conflict between North and South Korea, they feared for their son. Dreaming of raising him in America, and after waiting several years, they were finally accepted into the United States.

But nothing went as planned. While his mother schooled him on the violin, his father struggled to put food on the table. He couldn't keep a job because he fought against, in his mind, the permissive culture, fought against learning the strange English language, fought to make himself understood.

Tragically, Min's parents were killed on a back street in San Francisco by a gang believing the couple had money in their pockets as they returned from church wearing their Sunday clothes. Their ten-year-old son fled for his life, his mother screaming at him to run.

Her screams still haunt him.

Min was raised by a loving foster family. He grew up a respectful, hard working young man, a skinny, five-foot-nine, his black hair trimmed to shoulder length. He married Charisa, a woman he fell passionately in love with while working his way through college. When Charisa became pregnant, he dropped out of school. Hearing it was much more affordable to live in Florida, the couple traveled from the west coast to the east coast ultimately settling in a little manufactured-home park in Port Orange. Once in awhile Min snuck into a nearby park late at night and played the violin, fantasized he was playing with his mother and father—Tchaikovsky, Chopin, Mozart.

Paradise it was not.

Charisa's love for Min waned during her pregnancy, their fights escalating after Richard was born. One day Min returned home from work to find a note. Charisa was sorry, but she loved someone else and was leaving him to cope with raising their son. She hoped Richard would forgive her some day.

Min's life had turned sour.

He started to drink, not a lot but enough to ease the pain of losing his sweetheart. He had worked up to manager of a 7/Eleven. He didn't like the job, but at least he'd been able to earn enough for his family to live on. Not long after Charisa left Min lost his job. When he was let go, he picked up some part-time work with a landscaper but with the downturn in the economy people mowed their own lawns. He tried to find work but it seemed no one wanted a laid-off gas-station attendant or a part-time gardener. That's what they called him.

Where had his dreams gone? Dreams of one day following in his parent's footsteps, to play the violin, or his ambition to start a repair shop for musical instruments.

The last six years had been hard. Terrible. Richard, now seven, needed love not a father who only seemed to yell at him.

Min sighed, put the case on the counter and washed it off. It wasn't as heavy as other case. Picking up the two he went outside to his carport, the empty carport. He had turned his car in for a used motorcycle, a scooter really. It was all he could afford but at least he was able to travel to an interview. Soon he'd have to turn the scooter in and take the bus, the nearest stop a mile away.

The carport was constructed with a small shed at the back end where the previous owner had left a rickety workbench. When Min bought the house, his plan was to fix it up, so he bought a few tools at a yard sale—hammer, saw, and a drill as well as a rake. Maybe he would be able to add to them with what was in the heavy case.

Setting the two cases on the workbench, he turned the wheels of the locks, but he had no idea how to figure out the combinations. He decided to try another approach—muscle. He checked the corner of the shed for the crowbar that he had never used, and then set to drilling around the lock of the heavy case.

Sweat began running down Min's face as he tried to drill through the steel. Wiping his face with his bare arm, removing the salty sweat before it ran into his eyes, he continued to drill. Frustrated at his lack of progress, he picked up the hammer slamming a mighty blow to the lock. To his amazement it gave way where he had drilled. With the crowbar Min pried the top away from the bottom leaving a small slit. Still unable to make out what was inside, he reached for his flashlight and beamed it through the small opening.

He blinked.

Wiped his face.

Blinked several times.

He stood up straight, arms hanging down at his side—flashlight in one hand, crowbar in the other. He stared down at the dented metal he was battling. He dropped the crowbar and set the flashlight on the bench. His brows scrunched together, hands splayed on either side of the case he had tackled.

His eyes shifted to the second case.

Picking up the drill he set to work. This time the task progressed faster having learned from his first efforts. This time, he didn't stop with a small slit. Once he had enough holes he anchored the case on the floor between his legs. He hammered the end of the crowbar between the various drill holes, jammed the crowbar in the slit, rocked it back and forth until the top fell away and the contents fell out onto the cement slab of the carport—four gold bars and a large manila envelope.

Min anchored the first case between his legs, with renewed vigor he slid the crowbar again into the slit, yanking hard, one way and the other. The top finally gave way. Gold bars tumbled to the floor. On his knees, he stared at the bars, and then counted—twenty bars, twenty four with the bars from other case.

He stood, continued to look down, leaned against the workbench, then turned and opened the envelope. He removed several sheets of heavy paper, all identical with the exception of a number—Apple Computer stock certificates. The number of shares represented by the certificates ranged from sixty to over a hundred. The certificates were made payable to Mr. Mortimer Haliday or Mrs. Jane Haliday. Holding the sheets of paper his fingers began to tremble. He quickly returned the certificates to the envelope.

Reaching for the empty liquor box he used for trash, Min carefully stacked the bars inside, laid the envelope on top, and tucked in the flaps. He shoved the demolished cases under the bench. Racing into the house, he returned with a blue blanket and covered the liquor box and the two mangled cases.

Later Min robotically served Richard a frozen dinner of Mac'n cheese. He had checked the business section of the newspaper for the price of gold.

$1632 an ounce.

An ounce!

He could barely lift the liquor box.

He scanned the stock tables for the close on Friday of Apple Computer. $605 a share.

A share!

Thinking about the number of shares he had seen, he knew there were close to three hundred.

That night Richard dreamed of pirates and Min, well, Min didn't dream. Min didn't sleep. He had to find out if the gold bars were actually *gold* bars. Tossing and turning, sitting up in bed, lying back down. What to do?

Opening his closet door, shifting his shirts on the hangars to the side, he carefully pulled out his violin case. Playing the instrument calmed his nerves, gave him hope he could handle what life threw at him. Playing a sonata, the bow running vigorously over the strings, he decided what he was going to do Monday morning.

There were several pawn shops in town. He was known at one of them. After he lost the 7/Eleven job, he had had to pawn several items. He would take one bar to the shop. But he didn't want the owner to ask how he had obtained the gold bar, if it was gold. He figured it would be wiser to visit the shop down in Daytona Beach. Several of his buddies had told him about it when he first had to pawn a watch his father had given him. That shop wouldn't ask questions and if they did he'd say ... say what? Say, he inherited it from his grandfather.

That's it. Grandfather collected gold coins, turned them in for a gold bar when he had enough. What about the Halidays? First things first. The gold.

Min went out to the shed several times during the night. He lifted the blanket each time, opened the flaps, lifted the envelope, to be sure he wasn't dreaming. Each time he readjusted the blanket to be sure it didn't look suspicious.

He finally dozed off into a fitful sleep.

Chapter 22

Sunday, 6:30 a.m. – Day Five

Another Sunday.
Nothing different from any other day.
Peaches nudged Manny's leg. He automatically gave her a pat on the head, let his forearms rest once again on his knees, right index finger brushing over his moustache. Sitting on the edge of his bed, shorts and bare feet, he pondered his life.
What did normal people do on Sunday?
At the grocery store late yesterday he saw young girls chattering, laughing, planning to go the beach. Talking about this or that boy. A couple counted the steaks in their basket, went through the names of people who were going to eat the meat.
Peaches nudged again. Trotted to the door, trotted back to Manny. Barked.
"Okay, girl, I'm coming."
Manny pulled on his black running shorts and tank top, then the socks and sneakers.
Peaches whined.
"You're getting to be a real nag, you know that don't you?"
Out the door, to the dock, to the driveway, Manny put one foot in front of the other.
Peaches instantly took up where she left off the night before, tormenting every squirrel that dared cross her path.

Manny began to pick up speed then suddenly stopped, fished in his pocket for his cell and punched a number.

"Hey, Captain, I'm at the turn. You sleeping in? Just because it's Sunday you—"

"You're out of breath. Stop a minute. You doing anything today, I mean anything that can't be done tomorrow?"

"Hmm, well, what do you have in mind?"

"Get away, just you and me. The dogs, too."

"And exactly where did you have in mind … this getting away?"

"I don't know. Just drive. North. St. Augustine…the beach…lie around … turn our phones off … and no business talk. How about it?"

"Give me thirty minutes to shower and change. Maggie and I will be out front, the two with nap sacks on our shoulders, ready to run away."

Manny smiled as he slapped his phone shut.

"Come on, Peaches. You and I have a date."

The black SUV sped north on Interstate 95. The man and the woman, sunglasses, black trousers and shirts, were content to simply enjoy the undulating scene of old oaks, palms, horse farms, and cow pastures entering then passing from sight.

Peaches and Maggie sat looking out the back window, then gave up and went to sleep sharing a blanket.

Manny glanced at Liz, put his hand over hers resting on the side of her seat.

"Nice." He looked back at the road.

"Nice." Liz closed her eyes, leaned her head back. "Very nice."

Time past. The car continued to eat up the miles.

"I know a place where the dogs can run. A dog park. How about we stop there first, let them run off pent-up energy so we can tie them up while we have a picnic on the beach."

"Whatever you say, Watson. You're in charge."

"Then, Sherlock, we'll stop at a grocery store and pick up a feast. I keep a cooler in the back. Did you bring a bathing suit?"

"You say beach and I think water. Actually, I have it on. You?"

Manny chuckled. "Scary. Yes, and I too am wearing it."

The next two hours were spent at the dog park, then the grocery store, then a short drive to a secluded spot on the beach. A line of trees stood a few yards from the sand creating enough shade for the dogs and a bowl of water.

Trekking with a blanket, the cooler, and two bags of delicacies for lunch, Liz picked a place to settle—ocean to the east, and the dogs lying in the shade, tied to the trees, in the opposite direction.

"Last one in is a yellow-bellied gator," Liz yelled striping as she ran over the sand, her blouse the last piece to be discarded as she hit the water.

Manny was on her heels, his clothes dropping beside hers on the sand as he ran to catch her.

Laughing, they both shook their heads, salty water spraying in all directions. A wave rolled in knocking them over. Surfacing, Liz dove into the next wave, Manny right behind her like dolphins playing, they swam and dove into wave after wave, body surfing in on a big wave, turning, paddling out, riding the next wave in.

"Oh ... that's it," Liz said, Manny held her up, folding her in his arms.

"Whatta you mean, that's it?" he said conjuring up a shocked look.

"I need some food. I haven't eaten today."

"How come?" he held her hand as they trudged up to the blanket now in the shade of the tall oaks.

"Well this man called this morning, inviting me to run away. *Now*, he said. Sooo, now meant no time to eat."

Manny stopped, holding her hand out as he looked her over. "With that blond hair, you are a dead ringer for Marilyn Monroe. No more Sherlock for you, young lady."

"Okay, Tom."

"Who's Tom."

"Selleck. You're a dead ringer for him even down to the curly black hair on your chest."

"How do you know he has curly hair on his chest?"

"Curly black hair. Pictures. When I was growing up he and my dad were my heroes. Tom played a PI you know. You even have a moustache like his."

"Hmm." Manny pulled her hand to him, kissed her forehead, then her lips. Lifting his head, he looked into her warm, welcoming eyes. They embraced again, a long deep embrace.

Manny slowly lifted his eyes, his hand in her shiny gold hair, tucking her softly under his chin.

"I think we'd better eat," she whispered.

"I think you're right, Stitch."

The dogs had been beside themselves when they couldn't join their masters in the water. There was a leash law on the beach and being their owners were lawmen they had remained tied to the tree. They were now content to lie quietly. The fun seemed to be over.

Liz opened the box of fried chicken and a container of potato salad while Manny opened the wine and two plastic goblets that Liz said they must have snatching them from the shelf in the paper-plate aisle of the grocery store.

Tapping her goblet to Manny's she wrinkled her nose.

"What's the matter," Manny asked taking a sip.

"Not the same ringtone as crystal," she giggled.

"So, has business picked up?"

"I thought business was off limits? Mmm, this chicken is wonderful."

"Well, business like in Jane's business, but planning is okay."

"Well, there's always my old boss, Mr. Goodwurthy. Maybe I should check how he's doing."

"Goodwurthy PI Agency. I've heard good things about him. Do you like being a PI?" Manny asked scooping some red-potato salad onto his paper plate.

"Oh, God, yes. There's so much happening…the field is wide open. What with cyber crime, breakthroughs in DNA … the puzzle. It's all about the puzzle. Fitting the pieces together. I love it. But, sounds like your police work … well, not so much. Do you still feel that way or were you just having a bad day?" Liz asked holding her goblet up for more wine.

"More than a bad day. With the cutbacks, the red tape, regulations and new laws tying our hands … it's not the same. I envy your freedom."

"Ho. Freedom maybe, but you wouldn't envy my bank account. Want one of those fudge bars?"

"Thought you'd never ask."

Sipping the last of the wine, they gazed at the crashing waves rolling with the incoming tide.

"Beautiful isn't it. Like there's nobody else in the world." Liz turned her head to Manny. "Thanks for inviting me to runaway with you."

Parking in Liz's driveway, Manny let the dogs out. Strapping on his gun belt and picking up his cell, he wrestled the cooler out of the back. "There's enough chicken left for a couple of nights. You can put it in your freezer next to all those frozen dinners," he chuckled. "Let's divvy the potato salad. I could eat a gallon of it."

Setting the cooler on the kitchen table they split the leftovers. Both were tired but at the same time exhilarated with their escape from reality.

At the front door, Manny suddenly turned, grasped her shoulders, his face tortured. He didn't want to leave. He pulled her to him, their bodies melting together. The beautiful day had torn down the fences. Their passion flared, passion for each other, no one else. How had they missed it?

Breathing came in short bursts, his hands roaming down her back pressing her closer.

A cell tone.

Whose?

Manny's phone.

As suddenly as he had taken her in his arms, he released her.

"I love you, Elizabeth."

He turned, charged out the door, cell to his ear. "Yeah, I'm on my way."

Chapter 23

Monday, 5:30 a.m. – Day Six

The moon was still shining when morning newspapers were thrown from the driver's car windows smacking the pavement of residential driveways and businesses. The morning edition of the News Journal was also posted online. The classified section contained the following ad in the Lost and Found column:

Lost in the winds of last week's twister: holiday ornaments including a Christmas angel six inches tall, and a decorated Easter egg (Eggbert story character—webbed feet and duckbill attached). Also lost: a steel briefcase. If you find any of these items call 386-969-9229. Reward offered.

Chapter 24

Monday, 8:05 a.m. – Day Six

Monday traffic was building and the coffee shop in the little strip mall was doing a brisk business. Cars began filling up the parking spots in front of a line of offices to one side of the mall.

Maggie raced around the patch of grass next to Liz's small office unit at the end of the orange stucco building. A black feral cat hissed at the dog. The collie hastily retreated, squeezing by Liz as she unlocked her office door.

Juggling her briefcase, laptop, and tote with a chicken sandwich plus a thermos of coffee, Liz fumbled for her cell before the ringing stopped.

"Hey, I thought we decided not to mention the case," Manny said.

Hearing his voice woke up the butterflies in her stomach, her breath catching in her throat.

"Good morning to you, too. I included *A* case in the ad. It's not likely more than one will be found in the same place."

"I guess you're right. The reward is a nice touch. Peaches missed seeing Maggie this morning."

She could hear him breathing.

Okay, keeping it impersonal is he. Like nothing happened yesterday—only my whole world tilted.

"Maggie missed seeing Peaches and I missed seeing you," Liz said putting the conversation back in the personal column. "I was rushed this morning so skipped the jog. My parents and Aunt Jane dropped by shortly after you left" Silence hung in the air, his words as he left her at the door reverberating in her head. "Ah … ah … to discuss what steps she had to take to get her life back on track—insurance claims, should she look for a place to live in the same park, switch to a condo, or—"

"Did she tip her hand regarding her—"

"Heavens, no. She—"

"Stitch, if we're going to keep finishing each other's sentences, we'd better get together or we'll lose track—"

"Right. How about 5:30. The Port Orange dog park so Peaches and Maggie can socialize with other dogs. Don't forget, I'm a blonde. An undercover blonde."

"Believe me, I'm not likely to forget Marilyn—"

They were dancing around the hours they spent together yesterday, but more important the heat that built up during those hours and the flame that flared before his cell rang.

"Nor I, Tom."

What kind of a conversation is this, she thought.

"Can I talk to you face to face or do you want me to sit on the bench in back of you?"

"Same bench. Opposite ends," she said laughing. "However, could you leave your gun belt in the car? Goes along with being inconspicuous, unless you wear a jacket then it would—"

"5:30."

Chapter 25

Monday, 8:29 a.m. – Day Six

The diamond-encrusted gold bracelet sent off rainbows of light as the sun hit the stones. The gold burned hot on Johnny's wrist. It was a magnificent piece. After buying Hector's bracelet at the pawn shop he had stopped at the area's premier jewelry store to have it appraised—$155,000. Retail.

Johnny Blood folded the classified section of the morning newspaper, setting it down on the table. Lifting his head, he gazed out the café's window at the drivers heading to work as he sipped his morning coffee.

So, he thought, *the twister deposited the case in the ocean where I would find it on the incoming tide. Very poetic. And now the owner's looking for it. Probably frantic. Reward! I just bet there is. Eggbert? What kind of a joke is that? Ornaments? An angel? I'd better check the beach again. Trying to downplay the value of the case. Well, Mrs. Haliday, besides a nice retirement fund, you may have given me something else I was looking for. I think I'll use one of your gold bars to get the attention of the big man.*

It was time to get in touch with the king, Thornton Gaylord. Nickname: Thorny. He was not to be tangled with. He had been a member of Florida's Thistle Gang since he was a kid and by various means was now the king of the Thistles. Originally based in Miami, Thorny moved the operation to the Daytona Beach area. Miami was too crowded. Too many gangs. Too many hands eager for a piece of the pie. The drug pie.

Johnny pulled his cell out of his shirt pocket. Punched in a code.

"Whatta you want?"

"Hi, Carlos. Tell Thorny that Johnny's calling, as in Johnny Blood."

"He don't talk to you, Blood. I talk to you."

"Oh, I think he'll talk to me. Tell him I'm calling about gold. A gold bar. A $50,000 gold bar. But ... if he's not interested—"

"Where is this bar?"

"In my hand."

"Wait a min," Carlos muttered.

Johnny smiled, nodded to the waitress as she set his plate of scrambled eggs, sausage, and whole-wheat toast in front of him. He hadn't consulted with his boss back in Washington.

He took a bite of sausage. *Hell, Hendrix doesn't care how I infiltrate the gang, so long as I get close to the head man, suppliers, put together names with faces. Drugs. Dirty business.*

"Blood ... you still there?"

"Yeah, I'm here, Carlos."

"Wednesday. Noon."

"Come on, Carlos, that's two days from now."

"Thorny's in Miami. Back Wednesday. Be here."

Blood slapped his phone shut. *What do I care if I meet with him today, tomorrow, or Wednesday? The important thing is I'm meeting with him. Gives me a couple more days in paradise ... checking the beaches.*

Chapter 26

Monday, 9:00 a.m. – Day Six

A few minutes before nine o'clock Manny parked in front of Sammy's Pawn Shop and waited for the owner's assistant manager to open the shop. The humidity was rising again as the sun beat down. Manny lowered the window on Peaches' side of the car and she stuck her muzzle through the opening, nose twitching.

Manny absently touched the fur on her back. "Going to be hot today, girl. Maybe I'll stop at home, change into shorts before we meet Liz and Maggie at the dog park. Not exactly under cover ... I'll remove my cover," he chuckled. Peaches turned, gave a soft bark then again poked her head out the window.

A gray-haired man, ponytail anchored with an elastic band at the back of his head, parked his beat-up Ford coup at the end of the lot and shuffled to the shop door. Fumbling with a ring of keys, he finally decided he had the right one, tried it, tried another key and unlocked the gate with iron bars. He shoved the accordion-like barrier away from the door. Fumbling again for the right key, he unlocked the shop door and stepped inside.

Manny gave him a couple of minutes to turn on the lights and have a couple of draws on what Manny presumed was coffee from the extra large plastic-foam cup he had carried inside.

At six feet, muscular build, Manny presented a no-nonsense figure dressed in black, gun in his gun belt, as he strode into the shop.

The assistant manager shuffled quickly from the back of the shop to greet the man standing at the counter. "Can I help you, officer?"

"Yes, you can. I was in here a few days ago. Talked to Sammy. I don't know if he told you, but one of your regulars, goes by the name of Hector, an old guy, kinda scruffy looking, was found in an alley last Thursday morning."

"No, officer, he didn't tell me. But then I've been out sick the last few days. Sammy probably thought he'd call me this morning. But, that name is familiar. Not sure why. If you say he was a regular then he must come in later in the day. I can't place him. I open up for Sammy. Usually out of here by noon, or one at the latest."

"Well, he came in and bought back a bracelet from you. He came in Thursday to claim the bracelet and, from the log book you keep, Sammy found that Hector had dealt with you. Early in the morning. Probably when you opened."

"Let me look at the book so I can see which entry you're referring to."

"Here's a picture of the bracelet. Does it ring a bell?" Manny flipped open his cell and navigated to the picture Liz had sent him.

"Oh, well now, yes, I remember that bracelet. Couldn't believe that Sammy only gave him fifteen bucks for it. It was worth way more than that, in my opinion. But I would never second guess Sammy. When Hector came in I remarked that he was lucky no one had bought it, being it was such a beautiful piece."

The assistant ran his finger down the log. "Here, here it is, officer. He came in with the fifteen bucks. He seemed relieved when he put it on that it was still here."

Manny flipped to the picture he took of Hector at the morgue. "Is this Hector?"

"Oh, no."

"Are you sure?"

"Yeah, I'm sure. I remember because I couldn't figure why a good looking guy would pawn such a valuable piece. I mean he was wearing fancy leather shoes. Fifteen bucks couldn't have been more than peanuts to him, not enough to take a chance that he'd lose the piece."

"Other than the fancy clothes—height, hair color?"

"I'd say a little under six, maybe five-foot-eleven. Sandy-red hair."

"Hmm. Well, did this Hector give you any identification? I imagine you ask for ID."

The assistant sighed, closed his eyes, then looked at Manny square in the face. "Whoa, now, I remember the conversation. Did something I never do. He used the words you just used, officer. Said he was a regular, was in a hurry, left his wallet on his dresser. Asked me to check for his name in our records. 'Surely I'm in there,' he said. Wanted the bracelet, now. Yes, sir, I checked and saw that he came in several times a week, so I took the fifteen bucks and gave him his jewelry. He certainly wasn't old or scruffy."

"His story, leaving his wallet home, may have sounded plausible. But there is a problem."

"What's that?" the assistant asked.

"Hector was dead."

Chapter 27

Monday, 9:20 a.m. – Day Six

The coffee dripped through the basket to the pot. Richard sat at the kitchen table eating Captain Crunch cereal, swinging his legs under his chair. He looked up at his father shuffling around the kitchen. Min poured a cup of coffee then slouched into a chair.

He was exhausted but at least he had come up with a plan. The plan meant he had to go out of the house. For two days he had fretted over leaving the liquor box in the shed unattended. What if someone found it? But he couldn't take the box with him … on his scooter. *Too many buts and what ifs.*

Richard shoveled another spoonful of cereal into his mouth, chewed. "Father, are you going to take me to the park? They're having a free baseball camp. Please, can I go?"

Min raised his head. "Is Billy going?"

"He said he was. His mom is taking him and bringing him home. Would you let me go with him? They're leaving in thirty minutes."

"Yes, you can go with him. I have to run an errand. I'll be gone a few hours, but I'll be back before you are."

Richard was surprised. His father usually said no. Usually said no to everything since his mother had left. He wished she'd come back. Things were better when she was here.

Richard suddenly looked scared. Was his father leaving him, too?

Min saw his son stiffen. "Richard, I'll be back. I promise. Do you know Billy's telephone number?"

"Yes, sir."

"OK. Here write it on the back of the phonebook. I'll call to ask if his mother minds taking you with Billy."

Min placed the call and thanked Billy's mom when she said she'd be happy to take Ricky. Closing his cell, he turned and smiled at Richard. "All set, now finish your cereal and then you can run along. Don't give his mom any trouble. You hear me?"

"Yes, sir. Father, I heard music last night. Did you—"

"What kind of music?"

"A violin. Was it you, Father?"

"Yes. I was playing."

"It was pretty." Richard took his empty bowl to the sink then scampered into his bedroom. He dressed for the baseball camp, pulled on his sneakers, and was out the door with a wave to his father.

Min sat sipping his coffee in the quiet of the house. Swallowing the last drop he straightened up, took a deep breath, and prepared for his errand.

Min entered the little shop in the middle of a min-mall—Lester's Pawn Shop. He chose the shop because it was small, thinking they wouldn't ask questions. Depending on whether the bar was really gold, he could go to the one a friend had talked about. A better place than where Min had gone to pawn his father's watch.

"Hello. Can I help you?"

A lady with curly gray hair sitting behind the counter looked up at Min as he walked up to her.

"Yes, please. I have this brick ... I guess you'd call it a bar," Min said retrieving the bar he had secured in the inside pocket of his jacket.

The woman stood, cleared a spot on the counter and then placed a black felt mat down on the glass.

Min gently laid the bar on the felt. "My grandfather ... he collected coins ... gold coins ... at least he said they were gold." He laughed ... a little laugh ... a nervous laugh.

The woman said nothing. Reaching under the counter she picked up a small wooden box. A testing kit.

"He … my grandfather passed away. He left me this little bar. I guess he turned the coins in for it. Easier to keep track of." Another nervous laugh.

"I don't know if it's gold … looks like gold. Could you tell me? What would you pay me for this brick?"

"My testing acids will tell us," the woman said. "If your bar, scratched onto this testing stone, dissolves quickly with this acid it means the metal is of a lower karat than the acid being used. If it does not dissolve in the acid, the metal is of the same karat level as the acid, and … we have the answer. Looks like your grandfather turned those coins in for a high-quality bullion, 22 karat, Mr. …Mr.?"

"What's it worth?" Min asked looking at the drop of acid.

"Well, today's spot price is … just a minute. $1599.10. I pay spot," she chuckled. "A gold dealer will pay spot and take two to three percent. Your bar weighs one kilo—32.15 ounces. We're looking at $51,411."

"I see. Well, I'll be back. I don't want to part with it just yet. Grandfather … you have some nice instruments. That French horn is a beauty."

"I have a couple of noteworthy instruments. If you're in to jazz … great set of drums I can show you. With that gold bar you could buy me out. Actually, I'd have to refer you to a gold dealer. I'm a pawnbroker—small stuff. You should ask for the spot price—nothing less."

The woman looked back at Min but he was already out the door.

Min scooted around the corner and stopped. He pulled a little notepad from his pants pocket. His hands were shaking as he hit the end of his pen several times trying to eject the point so he could write. He quickly calculated that he had over a million dollars in a liquor box shoved under his workbench. He could hardly breathe, gripped the handlebars of his scooter, staring at the road as he scooted home.

The woman behind the counter at Lester's Pawn Shop looked at the card a police captain had left at her shop on Saturday and dialed his number.

"Captain Salinas."

"Hello, Captain. You stopped at my shop. You asked if anybody had come in with a gold bar—one or more, I believe you said."

"That's right. What's the name of your shop?"

"Lester's Pawn Shop. On Ridgewood. Daytona Beach. A young … well maybe mid thirties … everyone looks young to me these days," she chuckled. "Anyway, this young man came in … just left …with a gold bar. Pure gold. I tested it. Wanted to know how much it was worth and then walked out."

"Did he leave his name?"

"No. Seemed interested in a French horn for some reason."

"Can you give me a description?"

"Yes. Asian, not tall, probably five-ten. Nice fella. Seemed nervous."

Chapter 28

Monday, 11:20 a.m. – Day Six

Liz shut down her computer. Another case solved leaving only one open investigation. Of course, there was still Aunt Jane, but she wouldn't think of charging her. Working with her crazy aunt and her weird circumstances was fun. And, she had an excuse to talk to Manny. A warm feeling fluttered in the pit of her stomach. *A few more hours and I'll be seeing him. Maybe he'll stop at my house after the dogs run. Maybe he'll stay for dinner—there's still leftover red-potato salad in the refrigerator.*

She looked at her clean desk. No case files. No yellow pad with notes. *First time that's ever happened.* "If business doesn't pick up soon, Maggie, we'll be forced to give up this office. Move everything back home. Take the bed out. No more guest bedroom. Maybe I should do that anyway."

Maggie thumped the floor with her tail. They had just come in from a walk and didn't think she was going to get a chance to chase that chattering squirrel again so soon.

Now what? Liz thought. *I've dusted, filled and changed Maggie's water bowl twice, and cleaned off the desk. Maybe take her for another walk. Can't hurt to get some more fresh air. Fresh air? It's 95 degrees—hot and humid.*

Sighing, Liz pushed herself out of the chair, looked around, walked to the window. People ambling in and out of the mall's little shops. Nobody moved fast in this heat.

Manny, Manny, Manny. I love you, Elizabeth, he said to me. Love ... not to be taken lightly. Not to be given lightly. I didn't want the day to end yesterday. Didn't want him to leave ... the feeling of his arms around me. Just a few more hours ...

Her cell rang.

Aunt Jane's ringtone.

Saved by the bell.

"Lizzy, hi. I was wondering if you could spare me an hour?"

"I think I could arrange it. What's up?"

"I just had a call from the manager of Happy Days Estates. There's a house three blocks from mine, rather my cement slab. Came through unscathed he said. The owner hasn't been able to sell it, moved out several months ago, and now with the calamity of the twister he's frantic. He wondered if I would like to rent it until my insurance money comes through. Maybe even rent to buy. I don't want to ask your mom to take me over because she doesn't know about my situation, if you know what I mean."

"Yes, I catch your drift and, if you want me to drive, I can do that. When do you want to go?"

"Well, now, or when you can get away, dear."

"I can get away," Liz said looking at her blank computer screen. "I'll be right over."

With a sigh, she disconnected. "Come on, Maggie, let's go help Aunt Jane. She's always good for a laugh."

Picking up her shoulder bag her cell rang again. Manny's ringtone. Her spirits soared. "Hi, I was just thinking about you. Want to stop by my place after the dogs—"

"I can't make it today. Cop stuff. Robbery. Call you later." Multiple sirens were blaring in the background then silence. The call was disconnected.

Her spirits plummeted.

The house at Happy Days was perfect. After a long-distance conversation with the owner in Missouri, and their okay allowing GumDrop to come with Jane, Jane signed an informal rental agreement on the spot, and was determined to spend the night in the house ... back in the park. The manager said he'd have final documents ready by the end of the week but with Jane's deposit and the okay from the owner, he gave her the go-ahead to move in.

After all, move in meant buying a suitcase at Wal-Mart for the few items she had purchased since being homeless: a toothbrush and paste, a pair of shoes, and cat food among other things. The house was fully furnished, dishes, pans, flatware, so she and GumDrop could walk in and pick up their lives together. *Dear little GumDrop.*

Liz visited Michael's craft store for a Christmas tree. Pre-lit, the Christmas tree stood alone, out of season, in the store's foliage display.

By late afternoon, after a trip to her sister's to pick up her car, Jane sat demurely on a needlepoint chair and poured two cups of tea in the living room of her rental house. It felt like home—a mirror image of the one that had blown away. The same layout, same creamy-white walls. Of course, all the furniture was different, more upscale. Jane and Morty preferred to invest their money in gold and Apple Computer stock over plushy creature comforts.

She and Liz sat back, sipping their tea as they gazed at the new holiday tree, the tiny white lights setting the tree aglow. No matter the branches were bare—it was a start. Jane mentioned to Liz that if she ended up buying the place, the first thing she would do would be to move the safe-room to her new carport. Morty was right.

"Lizzy, what about giving a story to a television reporter? Maybe with a picture of my new holiday tree. Ask if anyone has found Eggbert. He's so cute. The angel, too. They would make a nice story don't you think?" Jane smiled, knowing that Eggbert was the guardian of a treasure inside his tummy. And then, of course, the Angel's halo—Morty's wedding band.

Liz glanced at her aunt over the rim of the china teacup. She was doing so well considering everything that had happened to her. Liz suddenly deflated. The last two hours were hectic but now Manny's call, that he couldn't see her today, popped back in her mind.

Maggie was lying in front of the new tree, head on her paws, eyes following the conversation between the two humans sitting in front of her. Standing, stretching back and forth, she trotted to Liz's side, sat down, and rested her muzzle on Liz's lap.

Absently, Liz stroked her dog's head. The black and white collie wasn't satisfied and nudged her hand.

"Maggie's itching to go outside and I'd better be running along. I think a story about Eggbert and the angel is a good idea. I'll stop by my office and pick up the scrapbook. They can take pictures at the station. Who knows, maybe it will make the six o'clock news. Or eight or ten, if they decide to use it."

Giving her aunt a hug, Liz and Maggie left, Jane waving to them from the front door of her new home in Happy Days Estates.

Chapter 29

Monday, 4:10 p.m. – Day Six

    Min wrestled against the values his parents had instilled in him and his own moral compass. Several times during each night, he had padded out on bare feet to the shed, peeked under the blanket hoping he had only imagined what was under the cover. But, each time the gold bars taunted him.
    Returning home from the pawn shop he was so distraught he began playing his violin.
    Richard peeked into the room, watched his father sitting on a stool then pacing to the window then back to the stool, the bow flying over the violin strings. The music was magical. Leaning against the door, he suddenly fell into the room landing at the feet of his father.
    Cowering Richard looked up from the floor sure he was going to receive a spanking.
    Min held the bow mid-air over the violin strings looking down at Richard. Tears began to flow. He wanted so much for his son, opportunities he never had. He was sure Richard had the aptitude, having seen him with a bow in his hand, drawing it across the strings. Only one time. Min had stopped his son, afraid he would want more. Min envisioned music lessons at the best schools—Juilliard, the University of Paris-Sorbonne. The means to make that dream come true sat in a liquor box in his shed.

Timidly, Richard wiggled around until he sat cross-legged in front of his father. He had seen him cry only once. The day his mother left. He reached up and touched his father's hand, his bow hand.

"Can you teach me how to play the violin, father?"

Min looked through his tears at Richard then set his violin and bow on the table. It was the only piece of furniture in the room except for the stool and a wooden chair Min had salvaged from the curb of a neighbor's house put out for the next trash pickup. Min opened the closet, knelt down and pulled out a small violin case. Laying the case on the table he opened it and caressed the gleaming wood of the small violin inside.

Min showed Richard how to hold the instrument, how to hold the bow, and how to reverently slide the bow over the strings. At first the screeching sounds hurt Richard's ears, but patiently, every so patiently Min worked with Richard, as his mother had worked with him so many years ago. The screeching noise began to give way to the beauty of a serenade. The following hours the father, sitting on the stool, and son, sitting on the scratched wooden chair his feet dangling, played side by side.

Richard had the knack of holding the little violin with his chin freeing his left hand for placement on the fingerboard. Min's chest filled with wonder as he witnessed his son's inherent talent for the instrument. Min marveled how his son instinctively had the delicate bend in his little fingers which Min knew was so important for balancing the bow. By the time Min tucked Richard into bed that night they were playing together, simple scales, and then a short piece, *The Elephant Parachutist,* a sequence of notes his mother had taught him.

That night was extremely painful for Min. His son had shown a remarkable ability to play the small violin. How could any father not keep what was in the case, what seemed to come to him as a gift? After all, the boys found the cases in a swamp. If they hadn't gone swimming, the gold might have remained hidden for months, years, forever.

But, there was the Lost and Found column in the newspaper and Min had read the ad. In his heart, he knew the case in the shed was one in the same. Min returned to the little room with the scratched stool and chair. He picked up his violin and played through the night.

Chapter 30

Monday, 11:00 p.m. – Day Six

The late evening news was due to pop on the screen any second. Star settled herself on her couch, leaned forward messaging her aching feet. She liked this particular anchor lady—young Hispanic with a brilliant smile.

The bar had been busier than normal. Between the butt pinching, strutting on spiked heels, trays laden with pitchers of beer, potato skins and French fries, she was more than ready for a rest.

"Good evening. I'm Juanita Riviera and this is your news at eleven. An unidentified body was found in a Daytona Beach alley last Thursday morning. Sources tell us they believe the man died of a drug overdose. They are still investigating.

"Tonight we have a human interest story. I'm sure you remember the twister that ravaged a section of Port Orange last week. At the time, we reported that two women were saved because one of the women had installed a safe-room in her carport. This same senior lady had what she called a holiday tree—a Christmas tree, fully decorated, that she left up all year to celebrate the various holidays. Hence, she calls it her holiday tree.

"When the twister tore through her street it swept away her house and everything in it leaving only a cement slab, and, of course, the safe-room. She hasn't been able to locate any of her most precious belongings. She even posted an ad in the Lost and Found section of the News Journal. But, as yet, she hasn't heard a word from anyone.

"She is asking you, our viewing audience, to please call if you find one of her treasures. There are many, but tonight we are highlighting two. The first is a golden-haired angel that topped Jane's tree. This was a special angel in that the angel's halo was fashioned out of Jane's late husband's gold wedding band. A private person, Jane asked that we only use her first name.

"Jane kept a scrapbook of every ornament she put on the tree. Here's a picture of the little angel on your screen. Next to the angel, is a picture of a little guy she's looking for—Eggbert, the storybook character. Isn't he cute?

"If anyone finds the angel or Eggbert please call the number at the bottom of your screen. She's afraid the ring is long gone, but maybe the angel landed in someone's loving hands. So, if you find either of Jane's little friends, please call.

"Now, for the latest on the political front."

Star snapped off the television and stared at the angel sitting on top of her TV set. She thought back to the day she found her. She was sure it was the afternoon of the storm. Everyone at the bar was talking about the twister. She even saw news reports on the big screen when she was serving drinks.

The news lady said the name Jane, she thought. *And the ring. I have her husband's wedding ring. Well, I have to call. It means so much to that lady ... only a few bucks to me.*

Star didn't write down the number that had flashed on the television so she looked in the phonebook and called the station. The girl answering the phone didn't know what she was talking about so she switched her to Juanita Riviera. The reporter was thrilled to receive the call and immediately gave her the number Liz had given her. Ms. Riviera implored Star to let her know if she indeed had Jane's angel. She'd like to interview her.

Star hung up the phone. Looked at the clock. It was well after eleven. *Better wait until morning ... on the other hand I could sure make that Jane person happy if I called now. But she's probably asleep. I'll call the number in the morning,* she thought, rubbing the toes of her right foot.

Chapter 31

Tuesday, 9:00 a.m. – Day Seven

The cotton blanket flew in the air. Then the sheet. Then Star bolted upright. *Something important. I have to do something important this morning. What is it?*

Her eyes darted around the room landing on the angel sitting on top of her television.

Was the angel smiling at her?

"Oh, yes, you little cutie. You're going home."

Swinging her legs off the blow-up mattress, Star stood, stretched, and then ran to the bathroom to take a shower. Feeling like a million bucks, she sat on the barstool at the kitchen counter, pulled the notepad in front of her and dialed the number that Juanita Riviera had given her last night.

"Jane speaking," Liz answered so startled, she almost dropped the phone. It was the first time anyone had called Jane's Business number.

"Hi. My name is Star Bloom. Are you the Jane the reporter said would be at this number?"

"Yes. This number was given to the reporter yesterday. Can I help you?"

"Well, I guess it's the other way around. I found your angel."

Liz gasped audibly into the phone. "Star Bloom, you are wonderful. When can we meet? Now? Can you meet me now?"

"Yes, I can. I tell you I was so excited when I saw the picture of your little angel on the screen. There she was sitting on top of my television above the picture Ms. Riviera was showing."

"This is so wonderful. Aunt Jane is going to be thrilled."

"Wait, I thought you were Jane."

"I'm her niece. This whole thing is overwhelming for her. She asked me to answer the phone. You're the first to call. I'm at my office, on Nova. Jane will be here."

Liz gave Star the address, and verified her telephone was the same one displayed on her cell. She didn't want to lose Star Bloom.

Liz closed her eyes, clutched her cell, "Oh, thank you, God. Thank you. Thank you. Thank you."

She opened her eyes hearing Maggie's nails on the wood floor as she pranced around catching the excitement. Liz punched Jane's number.

"Aunt Jane, you aren't going to believe this. Your angel was found!"

"Oh, my. Are you sure?"

"Yes. A woman. Her name is Star Bloom. She's on her way right now to my office. Can you—"

"I'm on my way, Lizzy."

Within thirty minutes Star opened the office door and stepped inside. She was holding the angel.

Jane's eyes misted seeing the angel in the young woman's hand, her hand flying to her mouth. "Oh, Lizzy, look."

Star apprehensively held the angel out to the lady with the pink hair.

Jane stepped to the young woman, wrapping her tenderly in a hug. Then it was Liz's turn to give Star a hug.

Star, who had never received such a greeting, hugged in return, dabbed her eyes as the other two were dabbing theirs. Jane gently grasped the doll, smoothing down her gold curls.

"Why, Star, she doesn't have a speck of dirt on her dress. Wherever did you find her?" Jane asked.

"Well, I got off early ... I'm a waitress at the Manatee Bar and Grill up on ... oh, it doesn't matter. Anyway, I crashed on my couch, my feet really hurt, and looked out the window. Something shiny caught my eye. Oh, here." Star dug into her purse and pulled out a tissue. "The ring." Star put the tissue into the pink-haired lady's hand.

Jane sucked in a breath of air as she carefully folded back the tissue. Morty's gold wedding band. Her eyes filled with tears. No misting this time. And, again wrapped her arms around Star.

Star patted her back until Jane stepped away.

"So, as I was saying, something shiny caught my eye. I went outside straight for the shiny thing. But, as I walked, it was the angel I noticed sitting on one of those palm branches, I guess they're called fronds. Then you can imagine my surprise when I saw the ring. It is rather large. Your husband must have been a big man," she giggled. "I had planned to see if I could sell the ring but when that nice anchor lady, Juanita Riviera, told the story about your husband's ring, well, I couldn't keep it. You know, it just wouldn't have been the right thing to do."

"Oh, my dear, you are quite a woman. Please, can you sit a minute? Tell me about yourself," Jane said.

The coffee pot played its tune in the little utility closet heralding its final perk. "Coffee anyone?" Liz asked.

"Yes, please, Lizzy," Jane said.

"I could really use a cup," Star said smiling as she took a seat next to Jane. "I was in such a hurry to get here that I didn't even stop at my favorite shop."

Two straight-back chairs faced an old wooden desk Liz had purchased from a secondhand shop when she opened her private investigator business. Liz took her seat behind the desk and the coffee klatch began with Jane and Liz staring at Star.

She briefly told them about her job and then swung into her dream of someday going to culinary school to be a pastry chef. Maybe even sell taffy made from a recipe her grandmother had given her when she lived in Atlantic City.

"Just last week," Star continued after taking a sip of coffee with a splash of cream, "I was at the beach, you know that area near Main Street in Daytona Beach ... where those shops and arcades are located?"

Jane and Liz nodded that they knew the place she was talking about.

"I noticed a vacant spot where a little man sold souvenirs. I stopped to inquire about the spot ... perfect spot to sell my red-and-white-striped mint taffy. I was lucky because the manager happened to be in. I told him I was just inquiring, but what would it take for me to sell my taffy in that empty space on the side of his area—he had a hot dog vendor, and a few of those pinball games. So, that's about it."

"Well, what did he say?" Jane asked. "Are you going to set up a little shop?"

"Oh, no. I couldn't possibly. I live on my paycheck ... actually tips, day-to-day, and I'd have to go to school first. One can't live on taffy alone," she laughed. "Besides the Hilton Hotel is just down from Main Street. Who knows—a pastry chef might be needed—I could whip up red-and-white-stripe taffy. Put them on the guest's pillows at night. Who says it has to be chocolate. But, it was fun to inquire."

"Star, culinary school—is there one around here? What's the tuition?" Jane asked, setting her empty mug down on the desk, her eyes intent on what the young woman was saying.

"Daytona Beach Community College has a program on culinary operations, baking and pastry specialization. Sounds fancy doesn't it? I sent for the catalog—three semesters, almost four-thousand dollars—way out of my league. But I have a jar, my grandmother's cookie jar. A big glass teddy bear so you can see inside. She gave it to me a few years ago filled with her taffy. That's when I decided I wanted to make her taffy as a business. She told me to shoot higher—be a chef, pastry chef with taffy my personal specialty."

"My dear, what if you had, say, four thousand dollars for the program, maybe an internship at a restaurant that could use your talent?" Jane asked.

"I rent a room near the beach—real cheap. You know, when the snowbirds are away rents drop, but I'll have to move in October. But what are you getting at, Jane? I don't have four-hundred let alone four-thousand dollars."

"When does the fall semester start—soon I expect?" Jane asked. "September?" Liz and Jane glanced at each other, both pairs of eyes flashing with a conspiratorial twinkle.

"Middle of September. But I don't know the exact date. Never asked because I couldn't sign up."

"What if an angel paid your tuition ... everything having to do with the school? You could keep your waitress job I imagine for your rent, or inquire about a part-time job in one of those Hilton restaurants. I know they have several in that same hotel. And, you can give them my name as a reference for what a lovely, hardworking, and above all honest and trustworthy young lady you are."

Star stared at Jane, stunned by her offer. "Am I dreaming?"

"No, my dear. The angel is *giving* you a chance to bring your dreams to life. It won't be easy. Lots of hard work. What do you say? Are you up for the challenge?"

"Oh, yes, Jane. You bet I am."

Chapter 32

Tuesday, 1:00 p.m. – Day Seven

A hint of Star Bloom's perfume lingered in the air. Liz smiled thinking about Star and how her aunt had come up with a very unique reward. Star had floated out of the office promising Jane she would call about registration details for the culinary arts program.

Liz put in a call to Mr. Goodwurthy. He wasn't available so she left a message that she had called and would call again. *Just as well,* she thought. *What would I do if he offered to take me back into his firm? On the other hand, how depressing would it be if he didn't?*

She hadn't cleaned up after her early morning meeting. Looking at the coffee mugs, sighing, she carried them to the sink in the utility closet. Catching her reflection in the mirror over the microwave she paused. "Now what?" she asked. "Call the bank, Elizabeth. OK, stop nagging me."

Tapping her pen on the desk blotter waiting for Betty Tisdale to pickup, she gazed at Maggie asleep on her big, pink, cushy pillow.

"Hi, Liz, I'm afraid we're at a dead end, but I want to talk to you about something. Can you come over?"

"Sure, gimme fifteen." Liz hung up, smiling. *Nothing like stirring up a little action,* she thought, lifting the straps of her bag to her shoulder. "Come on girl. I know a big old oak tree near the bank—plenty of shade and tons of opportunities to people watch."

Betty Tisdale moved the folders off her visitor's chair nodding to Liz to have a seat. "Excuse me, Liz, but weren't you a redhead the last time we met?"

"Yeah, well, I wanted a change." Liz laughed as she sat down facing Ms. Tisdale.

Tisdale opened a folder lying in the center of her desk. "We traced the transfers of your aunt's accounts to an account in the name of Stanly Gomez. A bank in Juarez, Mexico."

"Well, that's progress."

"Yes, but the funds were in the account for all of fifteen minutes. Cashed out. And, if Gomez ever existed, he vanished without a trace."

"What about the originating computer, the one the perp used to transfer the money?"

"Smart blonde. You know something about how the internet works. Yes, our techs were able to get that computers ID. It was a laptop purchased in Washington D.C. We think it's a government computer," Betty said looking up over her glasses.

"Government? Uh oh."

"We haven't been able to track where in the government. It was one of several thousand in a large purchase—"

"And, with their record keeping, the chances of our finding who it was logged out to, let alone which of the hundreds of agencies, will be a nightmare. But, on the other hand ... not impossible. Thanks, Betty. If we turn up anything on our end, I'll let you know."

With no desire to go back to her depressingly quiet office, Liz ran several errands including the grocery store for dog food, and then drove home. At least Maggie would be able to romp around the yard.

Stepping in the front door, her cell rang. It was Manny bringing a smile to her lips.

"How's my favorite redhead?" he asked.

"You forgot. I'm undercover but I'll forgive you. This time. How's my favorite lawman?"

"I didn't forget, Stitch. Just reminding you I haven't seen you for days. How about I pick up a roasted chicken and a bag of greens for dinner on my boat?"

"Manny, that sounds wonderful. I have a little story to tell you."

"Hope it's a good story. Jane?"

"Yes, and yes."

"I have one, too."

"What time do you want Maggs and me to show up?"

"Peaches and I are leaving now. Thirty minutes?"

"Thirty it is and I'll bring the bottle of wine that's languishing in my refrigerator."

"Well, Maggie, I think it's time to test this blonde rumor ... blondes having more fun."

It took her the whole thirty minutes to shower and change into a clingy, sleeveless, white-silk blouse over a pair of flared white slacks. She added gold hoop earrings and a delicate long gold chain. Slipping on her new gold, jewel-encrusted sandals, she strode to the kitchen for the wine. Taking a last look in the hall mirror, she smiled, touched her thigh for Maggie to follow.

Chapter 33

Tuesday, 6:15 p.m. – Day Seven

Manny stood at the rail of his houseboat.
Waiting.
Liz turned into his driveway. He seemed to glide up the dock to greet her but stopped dead in his tracks as she alighted from the car. Maggie darted out behind her to find Peaches.
Pleased with his reaction, she hesitated a second before reaching for the wine bottle. Drawing back from the car, bottle in hand, Manny had closed the distance between them and gently put his hands on her cheeks.
"Wow." He softly kissed her lips, then, taking her hand, twirled her around.
"You like?" she asked laughing.
"I like. Come on, dinner's ready."
Manny took the bottle from her, kissing the top of her fingers. Keeping hold of her hand, they strolled to the boat and stepped up to the deck.

The sun was giving up for the day, stopped pushing the temperature ever higher, which made for a lovely evening on the houseboat. During dinner and now sipping the last of the wine, they glanced at the dogs as they jumped down to the dock. They chased a couple of squirrels as they scrambled up a tree then chattered high on the branches mocking the dogs barking below.

Manny leaned forward, his forearms on his thighs, holding his wine glass in his hands. "I had a conversation with a couple today and suggested they call you for help."

"What kind of help?"

"They think they've been victims of identity theft. I couldn't help them. These days with the cutbacks, I can't have my team investigate something unless it's bleeding."

"That must be frustrating for you ... and your team. If they call, I'll be happy to check it out for them. Cyber attacks, computer security are favorites of mine—my passion really."

"Good. Hacking is becoming an obsession of mine, too. I'm trying to keep up with the various methods to block the attacks. Anyway, let me know if they call. I'd like to kibitz on the case with you. Also, yesterday, I had a call from a pawn shop. I visited several shops on Saturday putting out the word to call me if someone came in with a gold bar." Manny shook his head. "Still have a hard time believing Jane's story. Anyway, the pawn lady said an Asian man had come in with a gold bar. He gave her a cockamamie story that he had inherited it from his grandfather."

"Oh, Manny do you think—"

"I don't know. She tested the bar, told him it was definitely gold, one kilo."

"What did he say?"

"Nothing. He left the shop. No name."

Liz looked wide-eyed at Manny. "Did she say anything about his age?"

"Thirty something."

"I wonder if he found one of the cases." Liz turned, gazed at the river, the water, a gentle flow pushed by the incoming tide several miles to the east. She returned her gaze to Manny.

Leaning back in his deckchair, his eyes softened holding her gaze. "Now, tell me the latest story about your aunt," Manny said softly, still holding her eyes. Both were silent. Liz felt a flush rising to her cheeks. She put her hand to her forehead, again looking out to the river.

"Well ... first, let me fill you in on my meeting with Betty Tisdale—the bank lady." Regaining control her voice was steady. "She said they traced the money to a bank in Juarez, to an account under the name of Stanly Gomez."

"The money?"

"Gone. But this kind of ties in with the cyber espionage and the couple you mentioned earlier. The bank techs traced the computer used to transfer the money to Washington D.C. It was part of a government purchase."

"And?"

"And nothing, but they're working on it."

"That's all for the bank?"

Liz nodded, looking back at the river, now a dark bluish gray. A warm breeze wafted up caressing her arm.

"You had another story."

"Right ... you know that television spot, Aunt Jane's story about the twister blowing her holiday tree away?"

"Yes, I saw it. Nice job."

"Manny, a woman called. She found the angel and Uncle Mortimer's wedding ring. We met the woman at my office this morning. I'm still amazed at what happened. A whole different perspective of my aunt." Liz stood, stepped to the railing, looking out over the water rippling gold from the setting sun.

"What?" Manny asked joining her, his heart warming as his arm brushed hers. Manny ran his fingers over her shoulder, kissed her cheek.

"Uh ... yes ... well, the woman, very pretty, young, maybe mid-twenties, blonde of course, has this dream of selling taffy. Not just any taffy. Her grandmother's recipe for red-and-white- taffy. This young girl, her name is Star," Liz said rolling her eyes, "is a waitress at a bar up on Atlantic Avenue. She has no money. Lives on tips. But get this, Aunt Jane rewards her with $4,000. A reward so she can attend a one-year culinary arts program at Daytona Beach Community College specializing in baking and pastries." Liz beamed at Manny. "How's that for a happy story?"

"It is a happy story. Come here," Manny said. "You deserve a hug." He circled her with his arms, looked into her glowing face and was pulled again to put his lips to hers. The embrace grew warmer as she slowly encircled him with her arms, her hands resting on the back of his neck. Raising his head he looked into her big brown eyes, eyes that were soft and wanting. Lowering his lips to hers once more, the kiss deepened, his arms tightened, her body willingly met his. Holding her he put his cheek to her silky blond hair. She made no move to leave his embrace.

"Liz, I want to see you more often. It's been a wonderful … sharing dinner with you, swapping stories, sharing the evening. I want more of them."

He freed her from his arms, his hands brushing down her arms, grasping both of her hands.

Her breathing erratic, Liz took several deep breaths trying to calm her heart rate. Stepping away from him, she turned back, smiled, and planted a quick peck on his cheek.

"Captain, I'd like that very much—the dinner thingy."

Laughing, he helped her off the boat and with an arm draped around her shoulders walked her to her car. Maggie jumped in and barked goodbye to Peaches. Liz turned out of the driveway and disappeared down the road.

Her eyes misted. *What happened … or didn't happen. He didn't say the L word. Did I imagine Sunday. No. Maybe he didn't mean it. No, I'm sure he did.*

Pulling into her driveway, Liz opened the door and let Maggie out. She stayed in the car, looking up at the moon. She wasn't sure what Manny was feeling, but she felt weak, felt a longing so deep … was this what love felt like? If this was love, it was consuming her.

I have to step back. Be sure. Maybe that's what happened tonight. He stepped back to be sure. But, what if he decides he doesn't love me?

She got out of the car, pushing the button to lock it. Maggie sat at the front door waiting to go inside.

Chapter 34

Wednesday, 9:00 a.m. – Day Eight

The city had yet to pick up all the debris left behind by the twister.
Twister! Donald Sanderson thought. *It's a mean twist of fate, all right.*
He looked out the kitchen window at the remains of the branch stacked at the end of the driveway. If the branch hadn't blocked his car, he might have taken Bella to a different spot on the beach, and she wouldn't have found Eggbert.
Donald took his coffee outside, sat at the top of the ramp in the cool morning air. He had built the ramp to make the house wheelchair accessible when it became obvious Bella wasn't going to walk.
Sighing, he shuffled down the ramp in his bare feet. Walked to the end of the driveway and back. He hadn't told his daughter about the news report he'd seen on television two nights ago. The report of a lady looking for an angel and Eggbert. Donald had been agonizing ever since. He was sure the Eggbert doll that Bella found belonged to the lady.
But the diamond represented an operation for Bella.
Meant Bella might walk.
He closed his eyes, opened them, looking to the heavens. "God, what am I to do?"

Hearing a rap on the window, Donald looked up. Bella was awake. She had rapped on her bedroom window to get his attention. He waved and hurried inside.

Donald carried his daughter, Eggbert tucked under her arm, to the living room floor to watch her favorite morning cartoon show. The weather report was finishing as he snapped on the TV and the face of a smiling brunette news reporter filled the screen.

"Daddy, that's not the channel. Switch it, please, so I can see my show," Bella said bouncing Eggbert on her lap.

"Just a minute, sweetie. Let's see what the reporter has to say."

"Good morning. I'm Heather Colby. I have an update to a previous report that I think you'll like. You might remember the story about a lady who lost everything in the twister last week. She survived in the safe-room her late husband had insisted they install in their carport.

"The woman had a holiday tree—left it standing all year. The tree was swept away with her house including the angel that was perched on top of the tree when the storm hit. I'm happy to report that a young waitress saw our broadcast. She had found the angel, called the woman, and was rewarded handsomely for returning the precious ornament. But, the story doesn't end there. She also returned a gold diamond ring which turned out to be the wedding band of the woman's late husband.

"Doing the right thing pays, folks. The young woman could have sold the ring but because she returned it to the grateful owner. She received a reward that meant much more to her than the ring.

"Because the ring and angel were reported found as result of our broadcast, the woman wants your help in finding another ornament that has special meaning to her. It's an Easter egg. Well, actually, it's a storybook character—Eggbert. Here's his picture. If anyone out there in TV-land finds this cute egg, please call the number below so he can once again return to a branch on the woman's new holiday tree.

"Our next story—"

"Daddy, did you see? Did you see? Eggbert's mommy is looking for him."

Bella looked over at her father standing next to the television. He had a pen in his hand and was staring at the pad of paper where he had written the telephone number that flashed on the screen. He turned to his daughter. She was clutching Eggbert to her heart, her little eyebrows scrunched together.

"Daddy, do we have to give Eggbert back to his mommy?"

The story was out. Bella heard it. Now, Donald had to make the decision he'd feared since he first heard about the woman and her holiday tree two days ago. The diamond that had been placed in Eggbert's tummy for safekeeping represented the means whereby Bella could have the operation she so desperately needed. How could he give that up?

"What do you think we should do, Bella?"

"Well ... if I was lost ... and someone found me, I guess you'd want that person to give me back to you," she said straightening the tufts of hair on Eggbert's head, and then running her fingers over his soft webbed feet. A tear dropped on her pink flowered pajamas.

Donald rubbed his hand over his head, turning away from Bella.

Maybe we could just return the doll. Keep the diamond. No. The woman would know we found the stone. Of course, it could have fallen out. Don't be silly. She'd know I was a fraud.

"Yes, Bella, if you were lost I would do anything to get you back."

Donald sighed and picked up the phone.

Liz snatched Jane's Business cell off her desk. "Hello."

"Ah ... ah, my daughter and I just saw a news story on TV. About a missing doll. Eggbert. This number was given to call if the doll was found. Are you the mom ... owner, or did I write down the wrong number?"

"No, no ... I mean, you have the right number. Did you find Eggbert?"

"No ... Bella, my daughter Isabella did."

"How wonderful, Mr. ...

"Sanderson, Donald Sanderson."

"When can we meet you, Mr. Sanderson, and your daughter?"

"Well, we're home, so ... where do you want to meet?"

"Home, Jane's home. Let me give you the address."

"Are you Jane?"

"No, it's a little complicated. My name is Liz."

An old black Ford pulled slowly into the driveway. Jane and Liz peeked through the lace curtain covering the kitchen window that faced the carport. A man emerged, walked around to the back of the car and lifted the hatchback. A little girl waited in the front seat. The man pulled a wheelchair out of the back, snapped it open and wheeled it to the front of the car where the little girl was sitting.

"Lizzy, his daughter must be crippled. Quick, let's go to the door. The stairs. He can't wheel her in," Jane said hustling to the front door.

"Yoo-hoo, Mr. Sanderson?" Jane called as she opened the door, Liz peering over her aunt's shoulder.

The man looked up with a faint smile. "Hello. Yes, I'm Donald Sanderson. My daughter's name is Isabella. Are you Jane?"

"Yes, I am. I'm afraid the stairs will be difficult for a wheelchair. Can you bring your daughter—"

"I can carry Bella, if you have a chair—"

"Well, of course," Jane said smiling as the little girl's father lifted her from the car.

Clutching Eggbert, Bella's eyes were glued on the lady with the pink hair.

"Come on in. We'll sit in the living room."

The group trooped into the house after Jane. Bella's face lit up as her father sat her down on an overstuffed armchair facing Jane's holiday tree.

"You still have your Christmas tree up," Bella said, her eyes twinkling. "Is that the angel the lady showed on television?"

"Yes, it is Bella. She was lost, everything of mine was lost when that awful twister ripped down my street. Eggbert along with her."

"Oh. I'm glad you're okay."

"Tell me about yourself, dear. I saw your wheelchair."

"My legs don't work. They used to but not anymore. The doctor said he hoped he could fix them."

"She has a problem with her spine and needs an operation. I haven't been able to swing it yet," Donald said.

"What do you do, Mr. Sanderson. I'm Liz by the way, Jane's niece. We spoke on the phone."

"Nice to meet you, Liz. I'm a car salesman, or was. Lost my job when the dealership closed last month, which is why Bella and I were on the beach the day she found Eggbert."

Bella hugged Eggbert tight, gave him a kiss on his bill. "Here," Bella said holding Eggbert up to Jane.

"Thank you, dear. I'll put him up on this branch. Lizzy helped me pick out a new tree. I only call it a Christmas tree at Christmas time. Other than that, it's my holiday tree. Eggbert is for Easter."

"That's nice. Can we have a holiday tree, Daddy?"

"I think we might be able to do that. Mrs. ..."

"Jane Haliday, but I ask you to keep my last name a secret ... just between us. I'm a bit eccentric, you see—"

"What's essenric?"

"Well, some people think I'm peculiar. Different from most old ladies. Does that make sense, Bella?"

"I guess so. Like you have a Christmas tree in the summer?"

"Exactly, dear. Anyway, the nice television reporter agreed not to give out my last name. I don't want a lot of snoopy people coming around. So please call me Jane."

"Jane, I believe this also belongs to you." Donald reached in his pants pocket and pulled out the black velvet pouch. "When Bella found Eggbert, we, of course, didn't know about your loss. She was playing with Eggbert and we heard something rattle inside so I checked to see what was causing the sound and found the stone. I took it to a jewelry store where I bought my late wife's engagement ring. I didn't know if it was real ... so large. The jeweler said it was very precious and put it in this velvet bag. He told me the stone was a valuable yellow diamond. When we saw the news report, about you, and that you were looking for Eggbert, well, I was conflicted. I'm sorry to say I hesitated ... I prayed ... you see I was going to sell it so Bella could have her operation ... but it wasn't mine to sell."

Donald held out the pouch to Jane placing it in her hand. Jane released the gold tie, spread the top of the pouch open, and let the diamond roll out onto her palm.

Liz saw the look in Jane's eyes and knew what was coming.

"Well, now, Lizzy, what do you think of that?" Jane looked at her niece. They both were struggling against the tears gathering in their eyes.

"Mr. Sanderson, what's a seventy-year-old woman going to do with a yellow diamond? I think God meant for Isabella to find my Eggbert. You take it and get that doctor of hers to schedule her operation. And you, young lady, I have a pact to make with you."

"What's a pak?"

"It's an agreement between two people. In this case, it is an agreement between you and me." Jane plucked Eggbert from his branch on the holiday tree. "I agree to loan you Eggbert until the day you can walk up and return him to his branch on my holiday tree. I don't care how long it takes. I want you to have him, to keep you company through your operation, and all the therapy you're going to need to help you walk. I know it's going to be hard for you and your daddy. If you feel bad at times, you just look at this little cracked egg and know that if he can be made whole so you can you. Do you think you're brave enough to make that pact with me?"

"Oh, yes, Jane. And, I'll take special care of him, right, Daddy?"

"Right, Bella." Donald looked at Jane through the tears rolling down his face. "The two of us will take special care of him, and we promise never to tell Jane's last name. She'll be the lady with the magic holiday tree."

Chapter 35

Wednesday, 11:00 a.m. – Day Eight

What a great day, Liz thought, her lips drawn up into a smile from ear to ear. *Is it the sunshine? Little Bella? Maybe. But I have a sneaky suspicion it has more to do with last night.* Liz felt Manny's warmth again as he held her, kissed her. *Umm. I refuse to think any negative thoughts.*

Smacking the steering wheel, Liz looked into the rearview mirror. "Wasn't that little Bella adorable, Maggie. So poised and strength beyond her years."

Liz reached in her bag, retrieved her cell and punched Manny's code.

"Hi, Captain. Isn't it a beautiful day? Missed you this morning."

"Missed you, too. Called in on a case."

"I thought you'd like to know that Eggbert's back, or was, on the tree. A crippled six-year-old found her.

"Where?"

"On the beach, sitting in some grass."

"The diamond?"

"Yup. The dad performed a head-ectomy on Eggbert and out came the diamond."

Manny chuckled. "What did you mean by 'was on his branch?' Did he fall off?"

"No. Aunt Jane gave the diamond to the man. A doctor told them that with an operation he might be able to fix the little girl's legs. Who knows maybe he will. So, Aunt Jane loaned Eggbert to Bella until she can walk up and put him back on the tree."

"What a wonderful gift. What's on your agenda today?"

"Well, after that delightful evening, hard to top that, today I'm picking up Aunt Jane about six o'clock. Time to start up our evening WOW Club again."

"Let's see, that was Wine on Wednesday if I remember right. Of course, it was a candle-filled room at the time, and Jane was telling us about her millions."

"I guess the high-priestess was telling the truth," Liz giggled. "Today will be a little tamer I'm sure. We're going to the Daytona Beach Dog Track and Poker Club. That's a mouthful."

"Good luck … Stitch?"

"Yes, I'm here."

"I enjoyed our evening—oops, duty calls. I'll catch you later."

Chapter 36

Wednesday, 5:00 p.m. – Day Eight

The green truck barreled south on Interstate 95. Johnny Blood turned the radio up full blast, singing along with Johnny Cash—*Ring of Fire*. The meeting with Thorny went better than he could have dreamed possible. Blood briefed Hendrix, his boss in Washington, on his ascension to Thorny Gaylord's inner circle. Johnny didn't include in his briefing the importance of the gold bar he found.

Hendrix said that with any luck, Johnny could set up a sting on the Thistle gang in two to three days putting another drug gang out of operation. The sooner the better before Johnny was burned causing the gang to disperse yielding nothing for all their undercover work. Dismantling the gang and arresting its members would be a feather in DEA's cap. The Drug Enforcement Administration had been after Thornton Gaylord for a long time. They finally had an agent next to him as well as the names and pictures via cell phone of the gang's sinister tentacles.

Wednesday. A great day. Johnny believed he deserved a little down time, some fun.

Feeling lucky, feeling the Gods were smiling on him, Johnny decided a few hands at the poker table, and maybe a couple of bets on the greyhounds were in order providing him some deserved entertainment.

"Let's see how far I can stretch this winning streak," he said looking into his rearview mirror. The handsome sandy-haired man in the mirror flashed a wide smile showing his beautiful white-capped teeth and brilliant sparkling blue eyes in anticipation of a few hours of R&R.

Turning off the highway the truck sped along Williamson Boulevard to the Daytona Beach Kennel Club and Poker Room.

Jane hadn't been to the Poker Club for several months. She was especially excited about watching the greyhounds again. She wondered what GumDrop would think if she adopted a Greyhound. *Might be good for the both of us,* she thought. *Mix things up a little.* With the stress of the last few days, she felt a strong urge to go and place a few bets, kick up her heels so to speak, a stress release.

Before Morty died they visited the club regularly, almost every week. Maybe she'd get a sign from Morty that would clear the air, that she'd be all right, that the cases would show up, that he wasn't mad at her. She'd know right away, because when he got mad her dog never won let alone place or show. He was never mad at her, only himself for placing a bet on the wrong dog or a stupid bet on a possible flush at the poker table.

Lizzy was the only one she had shared her peculiar life with, so it was Lizzy she had invited to dinner to start up their WOW get-togethers for an evening at the Daytona Beach Kennel and Poker Club. Liz was aware that the club had built a new facility after they were squeezed out of the Speedway. NASCAR was now so popular that the two facilities couldn't continue to co-exist.

Stopping at a red light, Liz glanced at her aunt and smiled. The woman looked like a character out of a Broadway play, a lovable character wearing a dress with red-cabbage roses on purple fabric, and her ever present string of creamy white pearls around her neck.

"Aunt Jane, we're going to have fun. A great way to celebrate the return of the angel and little Bella finding Eggbert. As for the Greyhounds, will you give me a couple of tips on what to look for— which dog looks good or bad and why?"

"Of course, dear. But then you're on your own. Morty and I found that we had better results if we bet without collaborating. It always made for few arguments if my dog won but his didn't."

"I never heard you and Uncle Morty quarrel."

"We thought alike on most things, the big things—stock, diamonds, gold." She giggled. "Let's not think about that now. Let's have some fun, dear."

The club's parking lot was filling up fast. Mid-week gamblers hoped to fatten their wallets, sitting or standing outside in the late afternoon sunshine watching the races, eating a turkey wrap, enjoying an icy cold beer especially nice in the summer.

"Lizzy, I do like your hair. Exciting isn't it to change colors, gives a girl a lift. You should try pink sometime," Jane said stifling a chuckle.

"I'll think about it. If we win big tonight, maybe a nice green."

"I see the blond curls brought out more adventure in your clothes. That slinky black dress is going to cause some heart arrhythmia in the old geezers at the poker tables."

"You think?" Liz smiled at her aunt.

Following several men and a couple of women through the glass doors into the expansive lobby area of the club, Jane said she was going to check out the dogs.

"I'll join you in a few minutes, Aunt Jane. I'd like to walk around, take a peek in the poker room."

Several visitors were queued up at the information desk, their conversation animated as they peppered the two attendants with questions. Muted music was turned so low you had to concentrate to be sure you heard anything at all. Opposite the front entrance beyond a wide tiled area, were several rows of chairs facing a large bank of windows. Outside the windows was a patio with colorful umbrella tables, more chairs and then the dog track, a mile oval.

Liz had played poker a few times in college but had become a fair player under her aunt's tutelage on WOW evenings. Deciding she'd better watch the play of a few hands first, she slowly strolled around the tables, ovals seating eight players plus a chair for the dealer. Stopping at a table where all the seats were occupied, she stood to the side to watch.

A sandy-haired man sat two chairs to the left of the dealer, at the end of the oval. Liz stood behind a gray-haired woman, with numerous gold chains hanging from around her neck. The woman glanced at Liz, no smile, turned back to the table checking the card the dealer had just dealt in front of her, face down. The woman didn't like the card. She threw the hand down, shoving the cards away from her. "Not my day, Stan," she said getting up to leave.

Stan smiled at her and then dealt another round of cards to the remaining players. Liz stood in back of the empty chair and watched the play continue. The sandy-haired man checked his hand and slid a stack of chips forward into the pot. "Call and raise fifty."

All but two players threw their cards in and left. "Can't beat someone on a winning streak," one man mumbled as he edged out of his chair. He tapped the sandy-haired man on the shoulder. "Good luck to you, son. I'll be back when I see you leave," he chuckled.

Sandy-hair smiled up at the man and spotted Liz. "Hey, don't just stand there. Come join the party."

"Only observing, thank you. Besides, looks like I wouldn't have a chance with those stacks of chips in front of you," Liz said smiling.

"Ah. Not to worry. I'll spot you for two hands. Of course, you have to play as I say," he said flashing a smile at her. "OK with you, Stan, if I whisper in her ear?"

"As long as that's all you do, Johnny," Stan said retrieving the deck from the automated card shuffler.

Johnny looked at the two remaining players. They shrugged that it didn't matter to them if the pretty blonde watched. Stan dealt the cards.

Liz followed Johnny's instructions and earned a quick twenty-five dollars over and above what Johnny suggested she bet.

"Hey, I like this," Liz said smiling up at Stan. "But I have a feeling without my teacher here it might not be so fun."

"My name's Johnny. You are?"

"Elizabeth." Liz quickly shook Johnny's hand and nodded to Stan that she was skipping this hand.

A waitress stopped at the table and took a drink order from the other two players and then moved to Johnny.

"Elizabeth, can I buy you a drink. You've definitely added to my lucky day."

"Oh, thanks anyway, but I have to find my—"

Johnny reached for his cards, his shirt sleeve sliding back revealing a gold bracelet.

"That's a handsome bracelet you're wearing, Johnny." Liz looked from the bracelet to Johnny's face—a smile on his lips and a twinkle in his eyes.

"Like it? It was my father's. He gave it to me before he died. It's a beauty isn't it?"

Liz stood. "I think I'll take you up on that drink after all. Just give me a minute to tell my aunt where I am."

Chapter 37

Wednesday, 7:25 p.m. – Day Eight

Johnny's eyes followed the beautiful blonde's every step as she strolled out the glass doors of the poker room.

Spotting her aunt at the betting window Liz hustled up to her side. "Aunt Jane—"

"Just a minute, dear. I found a fine-looking dog. Betting on him to win." Jane handed the attendant two one-dollar bills. Plucking up the ticket the machine spit out, she smiled. "This is going to be a winner. I'll be back to collect," Jane said waving the ticket at the brunette who had entered her wager.

Liz tugged on Jane's arm, pulling her away from the betting window. "Aunt Jane, I just saw Uncle Morty's bracelet."

"What?" Jane whispered snapping around to face her niece. "Where?" Her brow raised, eyes wide, questioning.

"A man, playing poker. It was on his wrist. Could there be another bracelet like Uncle Morty's?"

Their voices hushed, they edged away from the crowd queuing up to place their bets.

"No. The jeweler designed it special for Morty. The designer was thrilled because Morty said not to worry about the expense. It was the year before he died. We were selling another batch of the Apple Computer stock and thought the bracelet a good investment. The only stipulation Morty gave him was that the diamonds be perfect, the gold of the highest quality for a piece of jewelry, and the onyx without flaw. The jeweler said it would be a one-of-a-kind piece." Jane took a breath and then spoke in a normal voice, scowling. "Lizzy, why are you acting so strange? This is wonderful. You found the bracelet."

"That's just it. The man said it was his father's. He's obviously lying," Liz said continuing to speak in a hushed voice. She stared down at the terracotta tile, arms crossed over her chest.

"But why would he do that?" Jane whispered inching closer to her niece, glancing left and right. No one was near them.

"I don't know why, but I'm going to try to find out. He offered to buy me a drink. I told him I was with my aunt and had to let her know where I was. I'm going back for that drink and then I'll come find you. And, for heaven's sake, don't come in the poker room and talk to me. There's no telling what I'll be saying."

"OK, Lizzy, but be careful. You don't know who this man is. He could be a robber."

Liz returned to the poker room and slid into the seat beside Johnny, smiling up at him with her big brown eyes. "I'm ready for that drink. Is the offer still open?"

"Of course, beautiful. What would you like?"

"If that's a martini you're drinking, I'll join you."

"Ah, a woman after my heart. Passes the first test—enjoys a real cocktail. Not a glass of white wine." Johnny flagged a waitress, pointed to his glass indicating another martini for the woman sitting next to him.

"Okay if I sit a minute, Stan. Watch how a master plays?"

"No problem. If Johnny says it's okay with him, it's okay with me," Stan said winking at Johnny and dealing the first cards of a new hand. A couple had replaced the two men who were playing before. They had just won big on a dog, a long-shot, and, laughing, had ambled into the poker room to try their luck. They were not serious players.

The waitress placed a martini in front of Liz and Johnny ordered another. Looking at Liz he tapped his glass to hers, sipped the last of his drink and pulled the olive off the gold-colored toothpick with his lips.

"What do you do, Johnny? Other than teaching a stranger how to play poker?"

"Import business … here and other countries. I'd like to retire and become a full-time poker player. Maybe enter competitions. You?"

"Sounds intriguing. I'm new to the area. My aunt lost her husband recently. You wouldn't know by looking at her, but she's not doing well, so I'm now her full-time companion."

"Does full-time mean you can't get away to have dinner with me tonight?"

"Um. Not tonight. But tomorrow night would work if you're here. I think I like this card-playing game … but I definitely need more help. Whew … the diamonds in that bracelet sure do sparkle. You say it was your father's?"

"That's right, honey." Johnny checked the card Stan dealt to him, and pushed several chips into the pot. The couple whispered back and forth, discussing what they should do. Finally, they decided to match Johnny's bet.

"Was he an importer, too?" Liz ran her tongue around the rim of her glass, at the same time sending a glowing smile Johnny's way.

Johnny placed his next bet, turned to Liz while the couple again whispered. "Dinner tomorrow night?"

Liz smiled, slowly drawing the olive off the gold toothpick, nodding, yes. Sliding off her chair, she thanked Johnny for the drink and turned away from the table as Stan dealt the next card in front of Johnny.

"7:00?" he called after her.

Liz turned, drew hers lips in a smile, mouthed, "7:00," and continued walking away feeling his eyes on her as she exited the glass doors to the track. She found Jane cheering on a doe-colored greyhound chasing the mechanical rabbit. On the way out, Liz brushed up against the waitress who had served Johnny his drinks.

"Excuse me, could you tell me Johnny's last name. I want to thank—"

"Oh, that's Johnny Blood. He's a regular."

Chapter 38

Wednesday, 9:05 p.m. - Day Eight

The silver PT Cruiser raced down Interstate 95, Liz's eyes riveted on the three-lane highway as it merged down to two.

Jane held tight to the roll-bar handle over the door. "What are you going to do, Lizzy?"

"I'm taking you home and then I'm talking to Manny. Give me my cell will you? It's in the side pocket," Liz said as she fished around the back of her seat, felt for her purse and handed it to Jane.

Liz flipped open her phone, glanced at the buttons and hit Manny's code.

"Hey, babe, how were the dogs?" Manny said.

"Can you meet me at my house ... twenty minutes? I'm on the road, dropping Aunt Jane off."

"Sure. You sound distracted. Heavy traffic?"

"I'll fill you in when I see you."

Liz popped a frozen pizza into the oven as Manny knocked on the back door and walked in. Peaches skirted around him looking for her playmate. There was an instant blur of black and white fur followed by all black as the dogs raced outside. Liz looked at Manny, his large frame filling the door, a bottle of wine in his hand.

A feeling of relief flowed over her. She felt a hitch in her stomach and a quick catch in her breath. She remained rooted to the floor. She didn't realize until that moment how much she wanted to see him, and he had come to her when she called.

Manny tipped his head a little to the side. Something was wrong. Setting the wine on the counter he gave her a quick hug and then leaned away. "I'll open that wine while you start filling me on what's buzzing around in that pretty head of yours." Releasing her after placing a soft peck on her cheek, he picked up the wine bottle, brows arched.

Opening the drawer next to him, she retrieved the wine opener and handed it to him along with a quick return kiss on his cheek. Flipping the CD player on, she set a candle on the table and lit it. She added two wine glasses, two small white ironstone plates, and a handful of white paper napkins. Concentrating on the table, she wrestled with bringing her breathing under control.

The flame of the candle danced to the music of *The Windmills of Your Mind,* windmills churning the bracelet with Johnny Blood, and now mixing with Manny's overwhelming presence filling her body. She watched him pour the wine handing her a glass, and then he sat facing her.

"Okay, what happened at the track?"

Liz took a deep breath, a sip of wine, and then began her report.

"While Aunt Jane was betting on the dogs, I walked around the poker room. I met a man."

"Oh, oh. I'm jealous," he said smiling.

Liz didn't return the smile, trying to collect her thoughts, trying to tamp down the feelings coursing through her body. She took another sip of wine staring over the rim of the glass at Manny. "This man at the poker table, he was wearing a bracelet. Manny, it was Uncle Morty's gold and diamond bracelet."

"Wonderful. But what makes you think it was your uncle's. From the picture, it's quite a piece. Could be more bracelets."

"I asked Aunt Jane that very thing. It's one of a kind. Designed special for Uncle Morty."

Manny opened his mouth to say something.

"Wait, there's more. He obviously lied. When I remarked about his bracelet he said his father had given it to him before he died. Why did he lie? He didn't have to. If he found it—wherever the twister had blown it, he could have said how lucky he was that he had found it.

After all, he didn't know there was any connection to me? No reason to lie?"

A scowl crossed over Manny's face as he looked down at the floor. Stood. Paced to the back door. Looked out as the dogs raced up barking, demanding to be let inside. He opened the door as the oven timer dinged.

The pizza was ready.

Liz pulled on an oven mitt, retrieved the pizza sliding it onto the butcher-block cutting board. "Sorry, I didn't ask if you had eaten. I was hungry. This is about the extent of my cooking. As I said, if it doesn't come in a box with directions to warm in the microwave or oven, I'd starve." Running the pizza cutter several times, she transferred the slices to a large platter and set it on the table. It was only then that she realized Manny was still standing at the backdoor. Peaches and Maggie had taken turns at the water bowl and were now stretched out on the brick patterned linoleum.

"Manny, come eat while it's—"

Manny turned around, scowling.

"What's the matter?" Liz asked noting the look on his face.

"The day after the tornado, I was called to check a body found in an ally. The guy died of an apparent overdose. He was a known addict. Remember when I called you to send a picture of your Uncle's bracelet?"

"Yes, you thought it had been pawned but someone had picked it up. This man?"

"Maybe. But when I showed the pawn shop owner a picture of the guy in the alley, he recognized him immediately, and said this was the guy who had pawned the bracelet. That's when I asked you to send me the picture. The owner looked at the picture and said that was definitely the bracelet that was pawned. That Hector, he's the guy in the alley, had pawned it late the day before just as he was closing for the day. The owner looked for the bracelet to show it to me but it wasn't there."

Manny paced to the door again turning to face Liz. "He checked the sale's log and said the bracelet had been picked up sometime around eleven Thursday morning—the day I was there but later in the afternoon. I had planned to stop at several pawn shops as I told you, to check if your uncle's ring or bracelet might have been pawned."

"Well, if Johnny, that's the man's name, found it and then bought it back why would he say ... I don't understand ..."

"The man you met didn't pawn the bracelet. Hector pawned it and he couldn't have bought it back because he was dead."

"Do you think this Hector guy gave Johnny the pawn ticket? Maybe for a fix? A fix that killed him?"

"I don't know. Could be drugs I guess. But somehow that bracelet turned up on this Johnny guy's wrist and it didn't come from his father. Did he give you his last name?"

"No, but when I was leaving I asked the waitress for his name. He bought me a drink and—"

"Oh, oh. Jealous again," Manny said, this time replacing the frown with a smile as he slid onto the chair, served a slice of pizza to Liz, then slid a piece onto his plate. After topping off their wine glasses, he tapped his to hers. "Here's to solving the mystery of your uncle's bracelet."

Liz sighed, took a bite of pizza. "Well, I'm having dinner with Johnny Blood, that's his name, tomorrow night at the Poker Club. I want to bleed him for information," she chuckled at the play of words on his name. "Let's come up with some questions I can thread into the conversation."

"Now, I am jealous. I'm coming with you—you're bodyguard."

"Don't be silly. But I know one thing for sure."

"What's that—this pizza's good. I didn't realize I was so hungry," Manny said.

"You worked up an appetite with all of those scowls trying to figure out how the pieces of the puzzle fit together. As I was saying, I know one thing I'm going to do and that's take a picture of Johnny with my cell."

"Oh, yah, you're going to say, 'I'd like to take your picture, say cheese, and by the way I know your father didn't give you that bracelet.'"

"Well, not exactly, but ... oh, oh, what am I going to wear? Maybe the outfit I wore when we had dinner on your boat. I have to admit I was trying to get your attention."

"It worked. You had my full attention from the moment you stepped out of your car. That's quite an outfit. I hoped it was just for me."

"It was, is ... but now I have a job to do. I just hope I can get Johnny's attention so I catch him unaware of what he's saying."

"I'm still going ... observing from the bar. I'll take his picture."

Liz walked with Manny to the backdoor, the dogs rushing out for a final romp. Standing in the shadows, music from the radio floated around them, *Sometimes When We Touch*. Manny slowly drew Liz into his arms, holding her head to his chest.

"Be careful tomorrow night," he whispered. Placing his fingers under her chin, he gently lifted her face to his. The kiss was warm, lingering, familiar. Feeling their hearts race in rhythm he leaned away, placed his lips to her forehead and left.

Chapter 39

Thursday, 6:00 a.m. – Day Nine

Unable to sleep Manny threw off the sheet and dressed. Skipping his morning jog, he drove directly to his office stopping only for a large Dunkin coffee. He was early. Way early. Something wasn't adding up and he was going to use all the resources of the Daytona Beach Police Department to find some answers.

He came up empty.

There wasn't a trace of a Johnny Blood in Daytona Beach, Volusia County, or all of Florida.

Who was this guy?

Why would he lie about the bracelet and what was his connection to Hector? Drugs?

As head of CID, Daytona Beach Criminal Investigation Department, Manny was pretty well plugged in with the Feds. Setting his third cup of coffee on his desk blotter, he called a friend of his in Washington. He told his friend he had some suspicions of a man by the name of Johnny Blood. Did he know the name? Manny said he was about to bring Blood in for questioning—he had a dead man in the morgue that may or may not have been an overdose victim. There was a tie to Blood.

Transferred twice, Manny was then instructed to hang up and wait for a call back.

Ten minutes past.

Manny's phone rang. The desk sergeant transferred the call. The call was from Washington D.C.

A male voice instructed Manny to hang on for Director Hendrix, DEA.

Manny was stunned at the conversation that followed.

First, he was told not to divulge what he was about to hear to anyone.

Second, there was a sting operation in progress initiated by the Miami office. And, yes, Agent Johnny Blood was undercover and had infiltrated the gang.

And, MANNY WAS TO STAND DOWN! It looked like the operation would wrap up in two days. He would be informed. Again, Hendrix said "Stand down."

"OK, OK, I hear you." Manny slowly placed the receiver in its cradle.

"No law against finding a pawn ticket," he mumbled. "Impersonating someone may or may not be illegal." He swallowed the last drop of his coffee. Threw the cup in the wastebasket. "Maybe Hector was killed by the gang."

Manny leaned back in his chair. Peaches got up, put her muzzle on his thigh. Manny stroked her silky head.

Now what am I going to do? I can't tell Liz this Blood guy is legit and in fact an agent. She might compromise his mission. Get shot in a crossfire. I have to keep my eyes on her tonight.

Chapter 40

Thursday, 6:14 a.m. – Day Nine

At the crack of dawn, Min once again shuffled to the shed, squatted down, lifted the blanket, and stared at the gold bars.

"Father? What are you looking at?" Richard had followed Min to the shed.

"Come here, Richard."

The little boy squatted mimicking his father, heads together, their inky black shoulder-length hair touching. Min put his arm around his son and lifted the blanket.

Squinting, Richard inched closer. "What is it, father?"

"Gold bars. They were in the cases you and Billy found in the pond. That's why the case you brought home was so heavy. Billy had four bars in his case and this envelope was in the bottom."

"What's in the envelope?" Richard looked up at his father.

"Stock certificates. When you invest in a company they give you pieces of paper to show you own part of that company."

With his small hand, Richard pushed against the liquor box but it didn't move. "Heavy. Must be a lot of gold in there. Whose is it?"

There it was.

The question.

Such a simple question.

Whose is it?

Well, Min thought, *the gold bars did not belong to Min Chong.*

"Come on, Richard, we have a telephone call to make."

The telephone number listed in the Lost and Found ad was different than the number he found in the phonebook for Haliday, the name on the stock certificates. Min picked up the Monday paper, classified section, he had put on top of the refrigerator. The telephone number was circled. Picking up the phone, he dialed.

"Hello."

"Ah … ah, hello. You … I saw an ad in Monday's paper. Lost and Found."

"Yes, you called the right number. Did you find something?"

"Yes, well, ah … my son found … my son and his friend found a couple of cases in a pond near us."

"Oh, my God. Yes … Mr.? What's your name?"

"Min Chong."

"Mr. Chong, my name is Liz. My aunt asked me to place the advertisement. She lost two cases last Wednesday. The twister—"

"Ah, yes. I guess they could be the same."

"Mr. Chong. Could you meet my aunt and I—"

"I don't have a car. A motorcycle. Really a scooter. I couldn't bring—"

"Oh, I understand. Can we come to your house?"

"Yes. That's fine."

"Where do you live?"

Min gave Liz the address as he stared at Richard. The little boy had a puzzled look on his face, his feet swinging back and forth on the kitchen chair.

"That's not far from where my aunt lives. OK if we come now? Thirty minutes?"

―――――

"Aunt Jane, are you dressed?"

"No, I'm still in my robe. What's the matter, Lizzy?"

"Oh, nothing … only that a man just called and I think he found two of your cases. Aunt Jane, one of them must have all those gold bars. Get dressed. I'll pick you up in a few minutes. He doesn't live far … just down the road."

True to her word, Liz turned her car into Min's driveway within thirty minutes. Before she and Jane could get their car doors open, a man and a little boy had stepped out of the backdoor and were standing in the carport facing the car.

Jane had on her lucky dress, purple with the red-cabbage roses, and a big smile. She hustled up to Mr. Chong, and the miniature Chong standing next to him. "I'm Jane Haliday, Mr. Chong, and this must be your son. You told my niece he found my cases?"

"Billy and I were in the pond. I thought I stepped on a dead fish," Richard said, his small hand holding tight to his father's hand.

"Oh, my. That must have been scary. Let me introduce my niece, Lizzy. You spoke with her on the phone, Mr. Chong."

"Ah ... yes ... I guess you want to see the cases. Richard found them last Sunday."

"Oh, yes, please," Jane said flashing a smile at Lizzy.

Min led the way to the shed. Richard ran by him and opened the door.

"It's very hot. No air conditioning," Min said. He bent down at the end of the workbench and retrieved the two mutilated cases. "Sorry," he said laying the cases at Jane's feet. "I didn't know what they were. I was curious. Forced them open."

Liz bent the tops back.

"They're empty, Mr. Chong," Jane said looking into Min's eyes.

"Yes, I transferred everything into this box." Min lifted the blue blanket, folded back the flaps on the box and handed the envelope on top to Jane revealing the neatly stacked gold bars.

"Oh, my. You are an honest man, Mr. Chong."

"It was my son, Mrs. Haliday. He saw me checking the box this morning. I was so worried that something bad might happen and I kept thinking it couldn't be true ... what was inside. Richard asked me, 'whose is it?'"

Min looked at Richard and smiled. For the first time since he opened the cases, he was at peace. "I knew they weren't mine. And, of course, the stock certificates had your name on them, and your husband's I guess."

"My husband died two years ago, Mr. Chong."

"I'm sorry it took me so long to call you. I saw ... circled, the telephone number listed in the newspaper, Lost and Found."

"Well, I think you two are just wonderful," Liz said giving Richard a hug, and, after a moment's hesitation, hugged a startled Mr. Chong.

"Can we chat a minute?" Jane asked. "I'd like to hear more about Richard's stepping on a dead fish. There are alligators around here you know," Jane chuckled.

"Yes, yes, of course, come in. Why don't we transfer the bars to your car first so you can lock them up. I have a couple of wastebaskets to help. I'm afraid the box will break apart."

Richard ran into the house for the wastebaskets while Liz turned the car around, and opened the trunk. With Richard's help, they transferred the bars into the back of the car, along with the beat-up cases. Liz covered everything with Maggie's blanket. Liz thought about her pooch. She looked so sad being left behind this morning.

Richard took Liz's hand leading her into the kitchen.

"Father's teaching me how to play the violin," he said beaming up at her.

"He is? Can you play something for us?"

"Can I, Father, please. We play together?"

"Oh, I don't know, Richard."

"Please? Stay here, Liz. I'll get the violins."

"Really, Richard—"

"Mr. Chong, Liz and I would love to hear your son play. From what he said, I guess you play, too?"

"Yes. A little."

Richard walked in with his father's violin case and handed it to him. Then he ran down the hall, and came back lugging a stool. "Father likes to sit on this when we play." Then he ran down the hall again and walked back with a small violin he had removed from its case. "I'll sit on the chair."

Min smiled at Richard, raised his eyebrows, and nodded to begin.

The sound was sweet, slow, measured. Then the bows of father and son began to sing in unison. Min nodded to his son keeping time with his foot, both with instruments under their chin, left hand on the fingerboard, bow hand in a delicate arch as they played the scales of the *Elephant Parachutist.*

Liz and Jane locked eyes. What's going on here? Do you believe this?

Crossing the strings one last time, they lifted their bows, smiled at each other and stood bowing deeply to their audience.

"Bravo. Bravo," Jane said bowing in return. Clapping.

"Wonderful. You are both wonderful," Liz said clapping.

"Put the violins in their cases, son," Min said. "Yours first, then come back for mine."

"Mr. Chong, you are a professional. What are you—"

"What am I doing here? Long Story. Short story, my mother and father played for the Seoul Philharmonic Orchestra. She taught me to play as a young boy. Same age as Richard now. They brought me to America fearing what was happening in Korea. They were both killed tragically in San Francisco. I went to university, married, and we had one son, Richard. My wife is gone and … here we are. I had hoped to play for an orchestra some day, or maybe start a business repairing instruments, maybe teaching."

"I would imagine you have the talent for both," Jane said. "What are you doing now?"

"I've had several jobs. Managing a 7/Eleven, mowing lawns, but nothing now … I'm trying to keep this house for Richard, but it's hard." Min looked out the window then turned back with a big smile. "It's only now that I find Richard has an ability to play the violin, my violin that my mother taught me how to play on."

Richard ran into the kitchen flopping onto a chair. "Did you like our concert, Liz?"

"I loved your concert, Richard."

"Mr. Chong, I'm sure you know the value of the gold bars that Richard found. It took an honorable man, and boy," Jane said looking at Richard, "to call me. As a reward, I'd like to supply the funds for your musical instrument shop, the business you dreamed of starting. And while I'm sure you are a wonderful teacher, how about finding a private school for Richard, one devoted to music?"

"Oh, Mrs. Haliday, your listening to our music is reward enough. I couldn't accept—"

"Nonsense. I'm sure your parents, bringing you to America, would urge you to accept my offer. You have shown your heritage—humble, honorable, strong family ties. Here's what I suggest you do. Find a suitable site for a small shop to begin your business. Probably in one of the strip malls. With the economic downturn there are many vacancies. At the same time find a school for Richard. How old are you Richard?"

"Seven, Mrs. Haliday."

"Well, if there isn't a school for your age, then a private instructor—perhaps someone affiliated with the Orlando Symphony."

"What about Billy. He was with me," Richard asked, his dark eyes wide.

"Richard, you're right," Min said. "We'll—"

"Tell us about Billy," Liz said smiling at the little protégé.

Richard put his head down. "Father, I told a lie."

"What sort of lie," Min asked.

"When you gave me the dollar to buy the case Billy found, I didn't give it to him." Richard jumped down off the chair, ran down the hall and back, stumbling into his father's leg. "Here's the dollar. I kept it."

"Why, Richard?"

"Because Billy's mother told him to put it in the garbage. So I didn't give it to him. I'm sorry."

Jane smiled at Richard, as he fessed up to keeping the dollar. "Well, Mr. Chong, you know the value of one of the gold bars?"

"Yes, Mrs. Haliday. A pawn shop owner quoted me $51,411 on the day I showed her a bar."

"That's about right. Here's what I'm going to do. Today I will give you three bars. Two gold bars are for you, Mr. Chong. Your startup capital. I expect you will need more to stock your shop, and then there's the marketing, and the fees they seem to levy on small business owners these days. Liz and I will stop by once you get set up to see how you're doing. And, by the way, if it turns out you want to do something else, no matter. The bars are yours and you can give whatever you feel is right to Billy and his mother."

"Mrs. Haliday, I cannot accept such a gift. It will be a loan and—"

"No, no, Mr. Chong. With due respect, the bars are yours. And the third bar is for you, Richard—a school, or whatever your father feels is best to continue to develop your talent. And, Mr. Chong, I have more than enough bars to fund Richard's future studies—be it in New York, Paris, or wherever his gift leads him."

"But, Mrs. Haliday—"

"No buts about it, Mr. Chong. Now, come on along, Richard, let's go out to the car and get those bars."

Chapter 41

Thursday, 11 a.m. – Day Nine

A spectacular day in paradise!

Johnny now understood why the country was tipping to the south, why seniors turned away from the banks of white snow to building sandcastles on the white beaches of Florida. Daily they flocked down to enjoy what the state had to offer. *Maybe I'll be one of those seniors in the years to come. But not quite yet,* he thought.

Getting close to Thorny had been easy. First, taking a little time to acclimate himself to the gang and how Thorny drove the operation. Befriend the lowest rung—hanging out with Milty. Then ingratiating himself up a few notches to Carlos.

Oh, yeah, it took chutzpa, a swagger to show he was tough, confident.

But then the big move no one else would have taken—buy his way in with a gold bar. Demonstrate he was a player. Wanted in on the action NOW.

He had spent the morning in a meeting Thorny called with all the key players of the Thistle gang, Thorny's inner circle.

"I charmed the pants off Thornton Gaylord," Johnny laughed, his fingers tapping the steering wheel, keeping time to Neil Diamond belting out, *Coming to America,* as he left the meeting, rolling down Thorny's sweeping circular driveway, lined with orange and pink hibiscus and stately palms standing as sentinels on either side. Johnny loved to sing—the shower, the beach, his truck. Had all the albums featuring Johnny Cash and Neil Diamond.

Thorny's mansion loomed large in the truck's rearview mirror, a pink mansion overlooking the white sand on the shores of the Atlantic. Even Johnny's green truck had made an impression—classy, tough in its understatement. No ostentatious black limo trying to mimic Thorny. No, Johnny Blood stood out, above Thorny's minions.

Johnny laughed again. What arrogance Thorny had to call a meeting with his top lieutenants, all gathered in the same place, same time. It was like picking lemons off a tree. One after the other Johnny built his list of thugs for Hendrix.

Thorny had opened the meeting by stating the real reason he had called them together. A large shipment of the purest, sweetest cocaine in the world was arriving from Columbia. The boat was slipping into the little-known marina, Ponce Inlet Harbor, where the SunCruz Casino gambling boat docked daily. A mid-size cruiser was not going to arouse suspicion.

Today Thorny had laid out the plans for his troops while sipping martinis on his veranda, bordered with bright colored Birds-of-Paradise and palmetto bushes. Explaining the operation, he waved his hand in the direction of the marina no more than seven miles away, a shipment that would arrive in the early morning hours—3:00 a.m.

Millions of dollars would change hands, the merchandise then fanning out over the lower forty-eight States. The millions would then multiply over and over again as the cocaine was divided into ever smaller packets, the number of packets multiplying again as did the money, a percentage going into the Thistle Gang's coffers each time a packet changed hands.

Thorny had taken Johnny to the side along with two of his most trusted men. Johnny and the other two were to take charge of the transactions as the boat was unloaded.

At the end of meeting a few gang members drove out of Thorny's driveway behind Johnny. They turned in the opposite direction. The remaining members had opted to stay in the opulent mansion, taking advantage of their host's hospitality.

Driving south on A1A, Atlantic Avenue, Johnny then turned west onto International Speedway. A few minutes later he turned again into the Volusia Mall parking lot. He continued on, away from cars parked near the entrances to Macy's, Nordstrom's, Sears, or the main entrance with access to the food court. He found a shady spot, parked, but kept the motor running. With the high heat and humidity the AC was a necessity. Sending an encrypted e-mail to Hendrix wasn't going to take long.

What a day!

Hendrix would act immediately, calling up agents from Miami, down from Jacksonville and Atlanta to get into position before 3:00 a.m.

Their adrenalin pumping.

The day, the hour, they had planned for was at hand.

The sting.

Bring down another monstrous warlord.

Johnny had grinned when Thorny told the men assembled before him that with this shipment he planned to expand the gang's tentacles.

Not!

Johnny shut down his laptop. Time for a little lunch, a nap after the long meeting, a meeting demanding Johnny's full attention—physically as well as mentally—then a shower.

Perfect.

As the red light turned to green, Johnny left the Volusia Mall and drove to a motel a few blocks from the poker room.

It was time to relax, concentrate on a certain gorgeous blonde.

He'd bided his time the night before, not rushing her, not being too aggressive, keeping his hands to himself. But that was going to stop. He could feel his heart rate accelerate just thinking about Elizabeth.

Meet for dinner. Take her someplace else. Too bright at the Poker Club. A nice romantic evening. Check her out. Suggest a weekend together after I close a big business deal. Ah, yes. A weekend with her. Maybe a month.

"I can afford it," he laughed.

Chapter 42

Thursday, 7:00 p.m. – Day Nine

Liz checked her image in the mirror as she attached silver tear-drops to her ears. "Whatta you think, Maggie?" she asked turning sideways, scanning her profile—backless heels, black palazzo slacks topped with a sleeveless, deep V-neck, silky-white blouse. "Will I be able to get some answers out of Mr. Blood tonight?"

Manny had called her several times during the afternoon requesting that she keep her radar up, urging her to be careful and finally pleading that she not get in the car with Blood. He didn't find any priors for the man. So, she quipped at the end of his last call, "He can't be a Ted Bundy."

With a pat on Maggie's head, Elizabeth Stevens picked up her small purse, dropped her cell inside, left the house and drove to the Poker Club.

The parking lot was over half full. A good thing, she thought. They wouldn't be alone. Besides, nothing about Johnny Blood the day before had set off warning bells. She only hoped she could find out why he lied about the bracelet.

Elizabeth spotted Johnny—light-blue cotton shirt, open at the neck, cuffs rolled up twice—just as he looked up. He was sitting at the same table he played at yesterday. *Was he watching for me,* she wondered? Out of the corner of her eye, she saw Manny move from the bar to a bank of betting windows at the same time putting his cell to his ear.

Johnny threw in his cards face down, pocketed his chips, and ambled over to Elizabeth, his eyes holding her in his.

"Hi," Johnny said placing a peck on her cheek. "You look beautiful, much too beautiful for dinner here. How about we mosey up somewhere on the ocean? It's a warm night." His hand lingered on her arm.

Manny had the picture he wanted. He turned away from Liz, walked out the front door, and placed a call to the private line he had been given this morning.

"Yeah."

"Hendrix?"

"Who's this?"

"Captain Salinas, Daytona Beach PD. We talked early this morning."

"You didn't make a move did you, Salinas?"

"No. You're message was received loud and clear. I just want to verify we're talking about the same person. I'm sending you a picture. Tell me if it's Blood. I'll hold."

A group passed Manny, laughing, joking about the killing they were going to make betting on the dogs.

"Yeah. That's him. STAND DOWN, SALINAS."

Johnny wasn't as tall as Manny, but Elizabeth, feeling the heat radiating from him, was suddenly a bit uneasy. *He doesn't know that I can deliver a karate punch to remove that grin from his face,* she thought. Manny's words rang in her ears, "Don't get into the car with him."

"Oh, let's stay here. I told my aunt I'd be back in a couple of hours. She's been sick all day but insisted I go out, at least for dinner."

"I'm disappointed. I'd like to show you off. I'd like us to spend more time together, get to know each other," he said placing a soft kiss on her lips. He guided her into the brightly lit dining room overlooking the track and to a little table for two tucked in the corner. Holding her chair, she graceful slid in smiling up at him.

A waitress hustled over with the menus and Johnny ordered two martinis. "I presume that's okay with you. You asked for one yesterday," he said reaching across the table for her hand, giving it a slight squeeze and then pointed to the menu. "Steak is their specialty. Of course, they also have fish." He ran his finger down the menu and then looked up.

"Steak is fine. I haven't had a *special* steak in a long time." She didn't feel like smiling, but gave it a try.

The waitress returned with their drinks, jotted down Johnny's dinner order, and left. He lifted his glass to Elizabeth's, "Here's to the first of many dinners."

Elizabeth lifted her glass to his and took a sip holding the speared olive to the side with her index finger.

"Before I forget," Johnny said with a chuckle. "Can I have your telephone number? What if I had to call you to change the time of our dinner tonight?"

Liz was prepared. She and Manny had discussed the possibility Johnny might ask for her number and they decided she would give him her new cell, Jane's Business number. She was already on alert when that phone rang so she wasn't apt to blurt out something without knowing who was on the other end of the line. Writing the number on her cocktail napkin, she slid it in front of Johnny. He grasped her fingers, raising them to his lips.

"I did almost have to change the time," Elizabeth said. "How can I reach you?" she asked sliding her fingers away from his, picking up her martini.

"Here's my cell." Johnny wrote his number and slid his napkin to her, opening his hand, inviting hers.

"Thanks. How were your cards falling today?" she asked ignoring his gesture.

"I didn't really get into a rhythm. Only been here an hour." He smiled, taking a long swallow of his drink.

"Duty called? You said you were in the import business. What exactly does that mean?"

"Not very exciting ... some foods, tobacco products, and some generic pharmaceuticals."

Their dinner arrived and Johnny ordered a second cocktail.

Taking a bite of steak, Elizabeth rolled her eyes. "You were right. This is delicious." She looked at Johnny. "Must keep you busy ... your job. That's quite an array of products. You must have to deal with several companies."

Johnny nodded, as he reached for the pepper his bracelet sparkled in the light.

"You don't have a southern accent. Midwest?" Elizabeth asked.

"Yep. Ohio. Parents were farmers. I got out of there as quick as I could. Had a stint in the Marines, and then when this job came along, I jumped on it."

"Have you always worked here, this area?"

"Only lately. Enough about me, Elizabeth. Elizabeth? You didn't tell me your last name."

"Elizabeth Stevens. I have to confess on my way out yesterday, when I was leaving, I asked the waitress who served our drinks for your last name. After all, a girl should know the full name of her dinner date, don't you think?" she said with a little laugh. Glancing at the other diners she saw Manny cutting into the house specialty.

Turning back to her dinner date, Elizabeth smiled. "You seem a little restless Johnny. Want to go back to the tables?"

"Not a chance. It's been a busy day … and now I'm sitting with a beautiful woman in this damn-bright restaurant. How about after dinner we have another drink outside? The sun has set so it should be cooler, however, looking at you … well, let's just say, I'll need a brisk breeze to cool off."

"A drink outside sounds delightful. It is bright in here."

They finished their steaks, and Johnny flagged the waitress, giving her the drink order and that he wanted the check. They were going to enjoy their cocktails outside on the patio.

Waiting for their martinis, Johnny nervously tapped the table with a spoon, looked up at Elizabeth smiling at him, and put the spoon down as the waitress arrived with the check and his order.

Outside, Johnny chose an umbrella table at the edge of the patio. The races had begun, a new race starting every fifteen minutes to the shouts and screams of the spectators pressing against the rail cheering on the dogs.

The table Johnny selected was far enough from the melee that the sounds of the crowd were somewhat muted. The scent of jasmine floated around the table from a cluster of nearby bushes.

"Ah, this is better," Johnny said pulling his chair closer to Elizabeth. "Here's to the beginning of a wonderful evening." He tapped his glass to hers, leaned forward his fingers slowly tracing her cheek. He caressed her hair, gently pulling her into his embrace and a soft taste of her lips.

The diamonds in his bracelet reflected the floodlights around the track as he lowered his hand to his glass.

Elizabeth released her breath. "You know, Johnny, I recognize your bracelet. I believe it's my aunt's." She said the words softly, letting them sink in.

"What?" He slowly shook his head. "No way, I found it. In a pawn shop." He took another sip of his drink. Leaned back, staring, holding her eyes again in an embrace. "Umm ... so beautiful." His fingers traced the inside of her hand then inside her arm to the crook in her elbow. "Next thing I know, you'll be saying I found a treasure chest with a couple of gold bars," he said his fingers running back over her skin to her palm.

"Funny you should say treasure chest. My aunt lost a chest in the twister last week. Blew her house away, all of her possessions. A chest. A chest with gold bars."

Johnny leaned back in his chair gazing into her eyes."

What's he thinking? Maybe going to admit he found the case. Oh, my God, he stole the money?

"Would you like another drink?"

"That would be nice."

"I'll be right back." He stood, raised her chin, kissed her lips. "Don't go away."

As soon as he disappeared inside the building, Liz fished her cell out, tapped a code.

"Aunt Jane, the case with the bank registers. Any gold bars?"

"Lizzy, why are you whispering I can barely hear you. There were two bars."

Liz slapped the phone shut, dropped it into her bag, watching Johnny through the window pay for their drinks. Thoughts spun in her head. Her heart began beating rapidly. *There are two cases unaccounted for. What are the odds that the one with two gold bars and all the bank registers were found by Johnny Blood? The bracelet is a separate issue. Highly unlikely it would have landed in the same spot with the case. On the other hand, the two cases Min Chong's son found were in the same pond, were feet from each other.*

Elizabeth stood, looked out at the track, looked at the screaming people as another group of seven greyhounds blurred in front of her.

Johnny came up behind her, set the drinks on the table, put his hands on her arms, caressed her arms, kissed her neck. Elizabeth turned, pecked his cheek and slid into her chair. Picking up her drink, she smiled at him, and took a sip. *I have to get out of here.*

Johnny sipped his martini, pulled his chair closer, his knee touching hers. His hand touched her leg, slid up a few inches to her thigh. "Elizabeth, come away with me for a few days. I have money. We'll charter a plane … go wherever you want … Jamaica, Columbia, Brazil. We'll leave tomorrow morning, early, six o'clock. More than a few days, Elizabeth."

He pulled her from her chair, held her against him. "Elizabeth, I—"

Elizabeth pushed gently against his chest, "I have to go. I don't feel well."

He continued to hold her, tighter.

She applied more pressure to his chest jerking free.

"I have to go."

Freed from his hands she grabbed her purse, walked quickly into the building, through the lobby, out to her car, and sped out of the parking lot onto Williamson Boulevard.

Chapter 43

Thursday, 9:00 p.m. – Day Nine

Tires screeched to a stop behind the PT Cruiser, headlights flashing twice.

Manny hopped out as Liz jumped from her car and ran to the black SUV throwing herself into his arms. He held her as he fell back against his car door.

Liz planted a short, but passionate, powerful kiss on his mouth, pulled back her head, her eyes shining in the moonlight.

"Now, that's what I call a greeting," he said moving in for another kiss.

Liz had other ideas.

Squirming from his arms she grabbed his hands, tugged and pulled him to the front door, releasing only long enough to insert her key into the lock.

"I have so much to tell you. You have to arrest him. Right away. I think something is happening tonight. He might be gone tomorrow."

She charged into the kitchen. Maggie barely got a pat but did get through to her mistress to let her out the backdoor.

"Arrest who?" Manny shouted shutting the front door, following her into the kitchen.

Liz was at the sink running water into the tea kettle. She whirled around. "Who? Where have you been the last two hours?"

"You know where I've been. The Kennel Club and—"

"Johnny Blood. I tell you, Captain Salinas, he stole my aunt's money. You have to arrest him."

"Whoa. Where did you get that idea?" Manny stood by the stove, hands on his hips, staring at the Tasmanian Devil whirling in front of him.

"I said to him … Johnny Blood … that's my aunt's bracelet. And he said, 'I found it.' I looked at him … but kept my cool … like yesterday. I said to him, you told me your father gave it to you. 'Oh, no, I didn't say that,' he said. I just looked at him. He looked at me and then he said that he supposed I was going to accuse him of stealing a treasure chest with a couple of gold bars. His absolute, actual, very words—quote, couple of gold bars, unquote. There were a few other words intermingled, but I caught the drift all right," she said slamming the kettle on the burner.

"Liz, how does that mean he stole Jane's money?"

"Manny," she looked at him with wide eyes, unbelieving that he was so dense, "my aunt has two cases still unaccounted for. Right?"

"Right."

"Johnny went in to get us another drink, probably to rearrange his thinking, what he was going to say to me, and I called Aunt Jane. I asked her how many bars were in the case with the bankbooks. 'Two.' She said, 'there were two.' Don't you see? I'm not saying the bracelet was in the case and I don't know where he found the case, or the bracelet, although, come to think of it, he did say a pawn shop. Maybe he is involved in your dead addict, that Hector guy. But … but, Manny, you have to arrest him."

Now Manny was pacing, rubbing his moustache with his fingers, looking up at her every time he reached a wall, turning in the other direction.

"The least you can do is bring him in for questioning," she said. "Tea? I have to have a cup of tea. My nerves are shot. I'll never sleep again."

Manny nodded at the teakettle, the whistle filling the kitchen suddenly silent.

Liz glared at Manny. He wasn't getting what she was saying. The urgency.

Manny paced.

"He made a move on me."

"I saw. I was about to arrest him for assault."

"Oh, swell, assault, but not for stealing several million dollars from my aunt."

"I can't arrest him tonight, Liz."

"Why not. I tell you he won't be here tomorrow."

"Why do you say that?"

"He asked me to go away with him, in the morning, six in the morning to be specific. That he had money. Don't you see?"

"I can't arrest him tonight, Stitch."

"Don't you Stitch me. I think you'd better leave. Go home and sleep on the idea why don't you? Here's his cell number," she snapped, slapping the cocktail napkin in his hand. "Maybe you can find it in your job description to saunter into the department about noon and ..."

She didn't finish her sentence. Manny had left stuffing the napkin into his pocket.

Nothing he could do tonight, but tomorrow morning he sure as hell could.

Manny backed out of her driveway, drove down the street to his houseboat to get Peaches and two thermoses of strong coffee. No, he couldn't arrest Johnny Blood tonight. He had been ordered by the DEA to stand down. But he was damn sure he wasn't going to leave Liz alone in her house unguarded.

He and Peaches were going to pull an all-night stakeout to be sure Blood didn't come for her. She hadn't given him her real name, or her telephone number, or her address, at least as far as he knew. But he also knew that Blood was a DEA Agent and it wouldn't be too hard for him to find her.

That was not going to happen!

Chapter 44

Friday, 6:30 a.m. – Day Ten

Manny poured coffee from his thermos into a cup as Liz stepped out of her front door. Maggie raced passed, circling Peaches. Leaning against her mailbox, Manny lifted the cup to her. A peace offering.

It was 6:30 in the morning. Time to jog.

Liz ambled up to Manny, looked at the cup, then up at his face.

"Sorry, it's all I have left," he said.

Liz glanced at the dogs chasing around the yard, glanced up the road at his SUV parked in the bushes, and then looked at the dark circles under his eyes. She took the cup he held out to her and sampled the tepid liquid.

"You were right," he said staring into her eyes. "Johnny Blood has disappeared."

"And, you know this because?" she asked leaning against her car that she had forgotten to pull into the garage.

"DEA called me an hour ago ... from Washington. What you don't know, what I was told not to divulge to anyone lest a sting operation be compromised, is that I also talked with them yesterday morning."

"I'm listening." Liz looked down, swiped the toe of her sneaker across the cement.

"I called the FBI to find out if they had a criminal record on Johnny Blood because of the possible tie between him and the dead guy in the alley, and the peculiar connection between him and the pawn shop and your uncle's bracelet. If Blood had a record, I was going to bring him in for questioning."

Liz dumped the remaining coffee on the grass and handed the cup back to Manny.

"Go on."

I was told that Johnny Blood was a DEA agent. That he was undercover in a gang dealing drugs in our area. I was also told that a shipment of drugs was expected to arrive early this morning and that Blood, through DEA, had put in motion a sting operation."

"But—"

Manny raised his hand. He had more to say.

"I was told in no uncertain terms to do nothing with Johnny Blood, to stand down, and not to repeat the conversation to anyone. That's what I knew last night. DEA called me an hour ago. The Director, a guy named Hendrix, wanted me to know that the operation was a success. Wanted to thank me for taking his words seriously. But, there was a problem."

Liz stood, arms crossed, listening, staring at Manny as he spoke.

"Blood has vanished with over a million dollars, some of the money that was to be paid for the drug shipment. Poof. DEA is looking for him but they believe he turned rogue and probably, some way, somehow, has fled the country."

Liz didn't say anything. She stared at Manny.

"You look like shit. Come on in. I think I have breakfast in the freezer—eggs, sausage, muffin—the works." Liz ambled to the front door. Manny followed dumping the remainder of the coffee, with coffee grounds in the bottom, on a flowerbed.

As Liz rooted around in the freezer for the frozen breakfast, her cell rang. It was Jane.

"Lizzy, you aren't going to believe what just happened."

"No, I probably won't, but try me," she said waving the box with an egg, a sausage and a muffin pictured on the wrapper.

"I just had a call from the bank. All my accounts have been fixed."

Liz's eyebrows shot up. Her head snapped over at Manny.

"What do you mean by fixed, Aunt Jane?"

"Why, the money, dear. It's all there—four million. Who says there no such thing as a miracle?"

Chapter 45

6 Months later

Sunday, 6:30 a.m. – Valentine's Day

Their feet slapped the pavement, matching stride for stride. Peaches and Maggie dashed one way, then another, then another. It was a brisk Sunday morning. Valentine's Day. Their jogging jackets had been tied around their waists a mile back. The vigorous pace warmed their skin, clearing sleepy cobwebs away.

"Coffee?" Liz puffed.

"Thought you'd never ask," Manny replied grinning.

"Your place or mine?"

"Mine."

Their gait slowed to a walk as they approached his driveway.

"Come here. I have something to show you." He took her hand, led her down a narrow path he had finished clearing the day before, led her to the middle of the slab where a house had stood before burning to the ground ten years ago. Manny bought the property soon after. The previous owners, devastated by the loss, had no heart to rebuild.

"It's a beautiful spot," she said.

Manny put his arm over Liz's shoulder as they gazed through the old oaks laden with Spanish moss. At one time several trees had been felled opening the view of the water and the dock from the windows that had once faced the river.

"It is nice," Manny said taking in the beauty of the land, of nature—stately palms, palmetto bushes, little purple flowers of Mexican Heather that had grown wild.

Liz looked up at Manny. "Have you finally decided to build a house on this foundation?" she asked picking a dandelion struggling to grow through a crack in the cement.

"I think so, but it depends," he said, his eyes dancing in the dappled sunlight.

"Depends?" Her brows squeezed together under her hand blocking a sunbeam.

"Yeah." Manny turned her into his arms, latching his hands in the small of her back. His dark brown eyes melting with hers.

"Stitch, I want us to build a home on this spot, to build a life together. I can't imagine a life without you. I love you. Will you marry me? Soon?"

Her lips parted, her heart pumping so hard she was sure it was going to pop from her chest. She raised her lips to his—warm, urgent lips, lips matching his with the warmth of her love. His lips that she had grown to wait for in the morning, friendly lips giving her a quick kiss as they parted for the day, kisses she yearned for at the end of the day.

Leaning back against his hands holding her, she smiled. "Captain, I thought you'd never ask."

Manny grasped her slim body to him, closed his eyes, the air held in his lungs releasing. Her head under his chin, her cheek to his chest, she looked out over the water, up at the trees, at the dogs barking at the base of a pine. "Manny, I love you with all my heart. Soon? Soon isn't soon enough," she laughed with a quick kiss on his chin.

Releasing one hand but still holding her with his arm, he dug into the pocket of his jogging pants. Removing a ring, he waved the beautiful solitaire diamond set in white gold in front of her eyes. "Now, you know, if you accept this, there's no going back."

"Hey, mister, put that ring on my finger. And as for the going back thingy, that works both ways you know."

Liz held her hand out in front of her admiring the ring as he slipped it on her finger. The diamond caught the sun's rays casting rainbows of light around them. Taking his hand, she tugged him with her to the edge of the slab, her hair's auburn strands glistening as the sun poked through the leaves swaying in a gentle breeze.

Threading her arm through his, she looked at the river, then up to him.

"Stitch, your mind is spinning—"

"Can we have a porch all the way across the front of the house? A door out of the kitchen for our morning coffee, and a door out the bedroom for a glass of wine in the evening?"

He laughed—a gentle tap on her nose, and a warm kiss on her forehead. "That's a wonderful idea."

"And, we can discuss our cases, well, whatever you can discuss, but I—"

"Ah, about our cases. I had a different twist to the word *our*. We don't have to decide right away—"

"What are you getting at?"

"What if we incorporated ... broadened what you do, add to the base of your investigations like cyber espionage, personal security and—"

"You mean like a Mr. and Mrs. Sherlock?"

"Well, if you put it that way, you'd have to promote me from a Watson to Sherlock."

"My God, this is wonderful. Two incorporations—you and me in business together, and, I can hardly say it ... you and me getting married." Liz threw her arms around him. "I love you. I love you. I love you."

Peaches and Maggie hearing her excited voice raced to the pair circling, barking. It must be play time.

Laughing, they released each other.

"Coffee?" she asked.

Grasping her hand he led her along the path to the driveway.

"This is going to be some Valentine's Day," Liz said, squeezing his hand.

"That it is, Stitch. That it is."

"Don't forget we're going to a concert, a matinee, this afternoon. What time should we leave? We have to swing by for Aunt Jane."

"Starts at two o'clock, so about 12:30?"

Standing on tiptoe, her fingers running through his hair, she pulled his lips to hers. "I love you and thank you for the beautiful ring."

Chapter 46

Sunday, 2:00 p.m. – Valentine's Day

Settling into their seats at the Bob Carr Performing Arts Center, they waited for the Orlando Symphony Orchestra to continue the matinee performance. Manny sat between the two women—Jane on one side, Liz on the other. His hand draped over the arm of his seat holding Liz's hand, ever so often raising it to his lips.

She turned her hand slightly in his, the diamond twinkling on her finger as the houselights dimmed.

Intermission was over.

The musicians were in place.

Two stools were positioned in front of the orchestra to the left of the conductor—one for an adult, the other for a child.

Min and Richard Chong emerged from behind the red velvet curtain.

Polite applause welcomed father and son onto the stage as they bowed to the audience of over a thousand. The program listed the special appearance of the Chongs as a father, Min Chong, with his child prodigy, Richard Chong.

Min began with a selection from Mozart's Violin Concerto No. 3, Rondo (Allegro) accompaniment by the full orchestra—a brisk, rapid tempo movement. At the conclusion of the selection, he lifted his bow, holding it a moment over the strings. The audience applauded, warming to the man.

Min looked at Richard. Father and son positioned their violins under their chins, Richard's eyes focusing on his father. The elder nodded. Raising their bows, as they had practiced, they played Camille Saint-Saëns, *The Swan*—slow, even, sweet—the music flowing over the audience seated in the red and gold hall. Both concluded at precisely the same moment, bows hovering over the strings.

Min immediately nodded. Richard raised his bow and played the same selection, *The Swan*, but this time solo. The boy concentrated as the bow caressed the strings, music flowing from the small violin. As before with his father, he concluded holding his bow, hand bent in perfect position, over the strings.

Richard had performed before his first audience, performed his first concert at the age of seven.

Min and Richard stood, faced their audience.

The audience, mesmerized at what they had just seen, at what they had just heard suddenly erupted in applause. Someone stood, followed by others, followed by the entire hall.

"Bravo. Bravo. Bravo."

Min and Richard bowed.

Min and Richard stepped apart, faced each other, bowed—father to son, son to father.

Chapter 47

Sunday, 6:00 p.m. – Valentine's Day

Conversation was light as Manny drove Liz and Jane back to Daytona Beach. The beauty of the music that flowed from the Chongs' violins continuing to envelope them.

Manny had invited the ladies to dinner, but they had one stop to make before celebrating their engagement with a bottle of champagne.

Walking down the hall of Halifax Memorial Hospital they heard the giggles of little girls. Stepping into room 413, Jane, Liz and Manny peering around her, saw four hospital beds—one was unoccupied, one had a little girl with her leg in a sling raised above her head, another lying flat her arm in a cast, and one lying perfectly still with Eggbert sitting on her chest.

"Jane, Jane, lookie, the nurse put a bandage on Eggbert's back just like mine."

"Hello, Bella, sweetie. I brought Lizzy and her brand new fiancé, a policeman, Captain Manny Salinas."

"Hi, Liz and mister policeman."

"Donald, how are you holding up with all these young ladies," Jane asked looking from bed to bed.

"Pretty well, thank you, Mrs. Haliday. As I'm sure you heard walking down the hall, spirits are pretty good in this room."

"Jane, meet my friends. That's Judy," Bella said pointing to the young girl with her leg raised. "She broke her leg trying to ride a bicycle. And that's my friend Callie. She broke her arm chasing her little brother around a swimming pool."

"And, Bella, how are you?" Liz asked planting a kiss on her pink cheek.

"Fine, I guess. It hurts a little, but the doctor said if I'm good and don't move around too much that in another few days I can go in the whirly water."

"Whirly water?" Liz asked looking at Donald. "The whirlpool—starting physical therapy. Nice to meet you, Captain, and congratulations," Donald said extending his hand.

"Daddy bought me a green bathing suit, just like Eggbert's."

"I bet it's real pretty," Manny said walking to Bella's bedside. "I seem to be a postman today. Here are three valentines addressed to Bella, Bella, and Bella." Manny smiled as he handed the envelopes to the little girl.

"Bella, do you want me to open them for you?" her daddy asked.

"Yes, please."

"Let's see, this one is from Jane … and this one from Liz, and look, this one is from your new policeman friend. He signed it Manny. All say, Happy Valentine's Day."

Jane smiled at Bella as the little girl examined the cards, showing each one to Eggbert. "Donald, how's your new job? I've appreciate your keeping me posted. The computer repair shop sounded interesting. Is it working out?"

"Oh, yes, Mrs. Haliday. I'd worked with computers somewhat before, before Bella was born. As I told you when I started with the shop, the owner thought he needed someone part time, but it turned out I knew enough to do the cleanup work, take care of any walk-ins and now he's training me to load software as well as some troubleshooting. He's still doing all the electrical work. What's nice is that my hours are flexible. With the lady next door taking care of Bella during most of the day, I can work at the shop. Sometimes I bring a system home to do the final cleanup so I can be with Bella."

"Sounds wonderful. Well, we have a dinner reservation, a celebration," Jane said winking at Manny. "Keep up the good work, Bella, and have fun in the whirly water."

"Bye, Jane. Liz, can you come see me in the whirly water? Daddy will let you know when. You can come too mister policeman. Are you going to marry Liz?"

"That's the plan, Bella."

"That's nice. She's very pretty. Not sure if I like the blond hair or the red better. Either way, she's pretty don't you think?"

"Bella, I think she's the most beautiful woman in the world, including you and Jane, of course."

Donald walked with Jane to the elevator. "Mrs. Haliday, again … thank you," he said his eyes filling up. "I can't thank you enough. Your generosity, your kindness—"

"Now, Donald, enough or you'll have me crying too. I'm just happy it all worked out the way it did. Isabella is a wonderful little girl. I'm just glad I could help and I believe the payments are up-to-date with her hospital bills. Now you get back in there with that precious valentine of yours."

Chapter 48

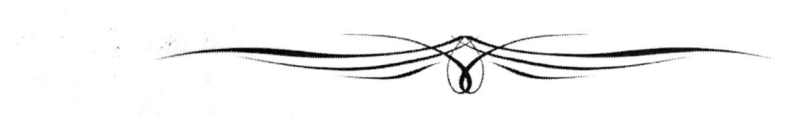

Sunday, 9:30 p.m. – Valentine's Day

The moon was shining, casting silvery shadows off the palm trees across the driveway as Manny parked behind Jane's car.

"I take it you like your new house, Jane," Manny said peering around the steering wheel at the safe-room. Construction had begun on framing in the iron box at the back of the carport.

"Love it. I'm glad I bought the place—same friends and neighbors."

"How about Mabel," Liz asked stepping out of the car and helping her aunt slide off the seat.

"She's still with her daughter, waiting for the insurance money," Jane said pulling her front door key out of her purse.

"Looks like you have two packages on your doorstep, Aunt Jane. Your neighbor signed for the big one. Left a note: 'Sorry I missed you yesterday.'"

"Please bring them in with you. Whew, it's been a big day. Can I interest you in a glass of wine?" Jane asked flipping the switch. A burst of tiny white lights from the holiday tree produced a cozy glow in the room.

Liz gripped the big box handing the smaller package to Manny as he already had a package tucked under his arm. He had been invited to join the WOW Club next Wednesday. "The day has been over the top so I couldn't wait to add to the festivities. I have a gift for you two founding members of the WOW Club. I have no illusions of my being a full-fledged member—'a part-timer' was how Liz put it. Nonetheless, I'm ready to present my initiation fee into the club."

Manny gave the box wrapped with gold paper and a satin ribbon to Jane as she settled into her rocker.

Jane pulled the end of the bow, the ribbon fluttering to her feet. "Lizzy, you open the rest." Liz took the box as GumDrop jumped up on Jane's lap, purring, nudging her hand to be petted.

Liz, cocking her head, smiled at Manny. "Well, let's see what we have here," she said ripping the paper away, opening the box to the glitter of three crystal goblets.

"Well done, Captain. I think this more than passes for your initiation into our club, don't you Aunt Jane?"

"Oh, yes, my dear. Beautiful goblets."

"The wine comes on Wednesday, but if you have a bottle in your cupboard, Jane, I think we can christen the glasses now."

"Splendid idea. There's a bottle of Pino Noir on the credenza behind you."

Manny opened and poured the wine.

Jane lifted her glass turning it in the twinkling lights of the holiday tree. "I propose a toast to Lizzy and her fiancé. May your love continue to grow and may your marriage be as happy as Morty's and mine."

The ring of crystal to crystal, a sip of wine, was followed with a kiss on each of Jane's cheeks from Liz and then Manny. Jane sat gazing through the crystal catching Manny and Liz in a warm embrace.

"Well ... I think we'd better get to those packages," Liz said placing another kiss on Manny's cheek.

"Aunt Jane, this smaller package is from Star."

"Open it up, please. When I went with her to register for the spring semester, she said the first class on the schedule was candy making. Maybe she sent me some taffy."

Liz removed the brown paper, revealing a shoebox with an envelope attached. She handed the card to Jane.

"It's a valentine." Jane's ruby lips turned up at the corners as she opened the card and began reading in a soft voice.

"Dear Jane,

Here's my prize winning taffy. Yes, I won the candy competition. Good way to start don't you think? Next is French pasty. Can't send that in the mail. I'll drop by so you can taste a sample. Maybe Liz can come over.

I mentioned to you when I was registering that I had applied for an intern spot at the Hilton—dessert sous-chef, well not exactly sous-chef, but I will be working with him. I started last week. They are so nice and try to schedule me around my classes. So, I quit at the Manatee. No more putting up with the butt-pinchers at the bar for this girl.

Happy Valentine's Day. Hope you like the taffy—give one to Liz when you see her.

Love, Star

Star Bloom

Assistant to the assistant dessert sous-chef at the Hilton Hotel"

"Now isn't that nice," Jane said opening the shoebox."That girl is certainly frugal and look at this—red-and-white-stripe taffy—all individually wrapped in cellophane with this pretty red satin ribbon. "

"Wait," Liz said, picking up a large piece of taffy. "She made three big pieces circled with red ribbon and hooks. The tag: *For your new holiday tree.*"

"How thoughtful. Put them on the tree, dear, and please get the little violins Min and Richard gave me for the tree. They're wrapped in tissue in my purse … on the credenza."

Liz retrieved the tissue. "They're so tiny, just the right size for the tree."

"The detail is extraordinary," Manny said. "I can only imagine the patience it took to craft them."

"There … how do they look, Aunt Jane?"

"Beautiful." Jane's face beamed seeing the new treasures on her tree, her hand running over GumDrop's soft fur. She plucked another piece of taffy from the shoebox. "Here, Manny try a piece of Star's taffy. And, then why don't you unwrap that other box for me."

Manny popped the piece of taffy into his mouth. "Umm, delicious," he said pulling up a chair next to Jane's rocker. "It's postmarked from Miami." Setting the large package on his knees, he tore off the brown paper revealing another layer of brown paper. "This is addressed to Mrs. Jane Haliday, Personal."

"My, my, very mysterious. Go ahead, tear that off, too."

Manny removed the second layer of brown paper revealing a heavy plastic green box, a bit smaller than a breadbox, with a white business-size envelope taped to the top. "Here, Jane you open it, your name again, and marked personal."

"Oh, it's a letter, handwritten, dated Christmas day, December 25, of last year. I'll read it to you."

> *"Dear Mrs. Haliday,*
> *You and I never met but I had the opportunity of meeting your niece, Elizabeth Stevens, a most beautiful woman. I had hoped for more than a brief acquaintance, but that was not to be.*
> *If you are reading this letter, it is because my dear friend, Carmelita, has carried out my instructions.*
> *I am living in a beautiful but dangerous part of the world. So dangerous that I know my days are numbered. The last few months living with Carmelita have caused me to assess my life, especially some of things I've done, in particular the choices I made this past August. This was at the time I met Elizabeth.*
> *I made bad choices. I did correct a big one—I'm sure you know what I mean. But even now I can't bring myself to right all the wrongs, to give up all that I found that morning sitting on the beach. However, if my final days come sooner rather than later, I showed Carmelita where this box is hidden, the one you are holding, and what she is to do with it should I be killed.*
> *So, Mrs. Haliday, if this box is sitting in front of you, it means the drug lords, who were always suspicious of where I came from, have killed me.*
> *Please tell Elizabeth I wished things could have been different.*
> *Sincerely,*
> *Johnny Blood*
> *Bogotá, Columbia"*

Jane exchanged a wide-eyed glance with Liz and Manny as Manny pulled his chair closer to Jane so she could open the box he held on his lap. No one said a word as she pulled the heavy tape from around the lid unsealing the green box.

Lifting the lid they saw three packages tightly taped with bubble wrap. Jane picked up the first, very small like a pound of butter, removed the plastic bubbles to another layer of heavy white paper. Tearing away the paper revealed a smaller box. She carefully pulled open the end shaking out the contents next to GumDrop. The box contained her four bankbooks, the instructions on sticky notes to access the accounts still intact.

Jane handed the box to Liz who put it on the lamp table beside her aunt's chair. "Well, I guess that clears up that mystery. You were right, Lizzy, that night at the dog track when you met him for dinner. You told me later you thought he stole my money."

"He must have restored the funds the morning of the sting. You were notified by the bank later the same morning."

Manny lifted the second box in bubble wrap. "Careful, Jane, it's heavy, like a five-pound sack of flour." He chuckled as GumDrop jumped down.

Jane removed the plastic wrap to a second layer of white paper. Removing the paper, a gold bar fell into her lap, another slipped to the floor before she could catch it.

"My God, Aunt Jane, he returned everything you said was in the case." Liz said looking up at her aunt.

Manny picked the bar up off the floor, shaking his head. "If you say that's everything that was in the case, what's in the last package?"

"It's very light," Jane said smiling up at Manny. "Of course, compared to the bars, anything would seem light," she giggled. "This is like Christmas."

Removing the plastic wrap, and the white paper, she was left with a black velvet box. "Now what can be in here … oh, Lizzy … look … it's Morty's bracelet," she said clutching the gold and diamond links to her heart, her eyes seeking the angel sitting on top of the holiday tree.

Liz topped off their goblets, and then she and Manny sat down on either side of Jane—the three staring at the holiday tree with the angel, Morty's ring circling her gold hair, the taffy and the miniature violins.

"Aunt Jane, you've touched the lives of some very special people."

"Oh, Lizzy, they touched my life. All they needed was a little love and a hand up. They could have kept silent, you know. But no, they were filled with the goodness of the human spirit. By being honorable they received more than the value of the items they found."

"But you helped them along, bringing their dreams within reach," Liz said. "Someday soon, I hope, a little girl will walk up and give you a hug as she returns Eggbert to his branch, and a young boy will give all of us hours of enjoyment through his music."

"Well, Jane," Manny said picking up the wrapping paper and bubble wrap, "I know you're still missing some of your holiday characters, but I guess you have the most expensive items that were blown away by the twister."

"Not quite, Manny," Jane said savoring a sip from the crystal goblet. "There's still a case out there. Twenty gold bars, one-and-a-quarter million, if my records are correct, and Morty never made a mistake. I wonder what adventure lies ahead?"

The End

Books by Mary Jane Forbes

FICTION

Murder by Design, Series:
Murder by Design – Book 1
Labeled in Seattle – Book 2
Choices, And the Courage to Risk – Book 3

Novel
The Baby Quilt … *a mystery!*

Elizabeth Stitchway, Private Investigator, Series:
The Mailbox – Book 1
Black Magic, An Arabian Stallion – Book 2
The Painter – Book 3
Twister – Book 4

House of Beads Mystery Series:
Murder in the House of Beads – Book 1
Intercept – Book 2
Checkmate – Book 3
Identity Theft – Book 4

Short Stories
Once Upon a Christmas Eve, a Romantic Fairy Tale
The Christmas Angel and the Magic Holiday Tree

NONFICTION
Authors, Self Publish With Style

Visit: www.MaryJaneForbes.com